SCHWARZENEGGER
END OF DAYS

UNIVERSAL PICTURES AND BEACON PICTURES PRESENT

ARNOLD SCHWARZENEGGER

A PETER HYAMS FILM "END OF DAYS" GABRIEL BYRNE KEVIN POLLAK ROBIN TUNNEY ROD STEIGER

DIR. PAUL DEASON ANDREW W. MARLOWE PRODUCERS STAN WINSTON GARY GOLDSTEIN STUDIO

MUSIC STEVE KEMPER SCORE JOHN DEBNEY MUSIC MARCO BELTRAMI

PRODUCTION ARMYAN BERNSTEIN BILL BORDEN PRODUCER RICHARD HOLLAND WRITTEN ANDREW W. MARLOWE

DIRECTOR OF PHOTOGRAPHY PETER HYAMS PRODUCERS MARC ABRAHAM THOMAS A. BLISS

EXECUTIVE PRODUCERS STAN WINSTON DIRECTED PETER HYAMS A UNIVERSAL RELEASE © 1999 UNIVERSAL STUDIOS

SOUNDTRACK AVAILABLE ON GEFFEN RECORDS FEATURING MUSIC FROM GUNS N' ROSES, LIMP BIZKIT, KORN, ROB ZOMBIE, EVERLAST, CREED

RESTRICTED R

END OF DAYS

FRANK LAURIA

Based on the screenplay by

ANDREW MARLOWE

St. Martin's Paperbacks

END OF DAYS

ISBN: 0-312-97262-8

Printed in the United States of America

St. Martin's Paperbacks edition / November 1999

10 9 8 7 6 5 4 3

In Thousand Nine Hundred Ninety-Nine . . .
A king of terror will come from Heaven

NOSTRADAMUS

PROLOGUE

Rome. The Eternal City.

Its ancient stones have witnessed man's vanities, lusts, triumphs, and tragedies for over two millenniums. Caesars, generals, and kings have all strutted in its glorious amphitheaters of power. But none were ever so mighty as the ruler of a small city-state within the protective confines of Rome.

From its modest hundred and nine acres, the city-state's authority encircles the entire world. And its rulers continue to prevail, centuries after the Caesars and kings have passed to dust.

The Vatican: sacred epicenter of the Roman Catholic Church.

Its prelates are the best, brightest, and bravest produced by the Catholic hierarchy. Its opulent salons are host to the richest, most influential—and most ruthless—men

on earth. Its magnificent cathedrals and li-
braries are vast repositories of arts and sci-
ences gleaned since the beginning of time.

But only a select few are privy to the inner
sanctums of the Vatican Library.

Not even His Holy Eminence, the pope,
knows the dark secrets guarded by a mysti-
cal order of monks, sworn knights in the war
against Lucifer . . .

So when the small comet first appeared in
the night sky, only these arcane monks
would understand the significance of the
rare celestial event.

But only one, a young ascetic named for
the visionary saint and philosopher, Thomas
Aquinas, could divine the comet's message.

Alone in a secluded garret that overlooked
the Tiber River, the priest pored over illuminated manuscripts and kabalistic scrolls
by the light of a silver candelabra. The dancing flames accentuated the sharp, hollow
planes of the young monk's face and the
fierce glaze of his gray eyes as he bent over
the precious documents.

Outside the open window, a full moon
hung low in the midnight sky, the comet's
tail arcing above it like a glittering eyebrow.

Wearily Thomas pushed away from the table and wandered to the window. For long
minutes the tall, emaciated monk stared
down at the marble angels protecting Cas-

tello Sant' Angelo. Thomas knew, with absolute certainty, that he had been chosen. But the thought that his soul was not pure enough to fulfill his ordained mission stabbed his belly with cold needles of fear. Thomas understood the horrifying consequences of failure.

He turned his gaze to the sky and prayed for inspiration.

Then Thomas saw it, in all its stunning simplicity.

The comet's bright tail curving over the full moon. Like a silver brow above an unblinking eye.

Feverishly Thomas hurried to a dusty bookshelf and rummaged through the leather-bound volumes. He withdrew a large, ancient manuscript and went to the table. Carefully, he leafed through the illuminated texts until he found it.

An ominous illustration of a full moon decorated the page. A sparkling comet streaked over the moon. The effect was that of a giant eye.

Thomas read the Latin words inked beneath the illustration.

"*Oculus Deum* . . . ," he whispered. *Eye of God*.

A psychic fervor overcame his exhaustion as he continued to read the text. Broken im-

ages fluttered through his brain like frightened birds.

They whirled faster and faster in a blurred,
flapping chaos until abruptly the fragments
merged into a single, mind-shattering vision
of unspeakable evil, and he fell swooning to
the floor.

Moments later, when he recovered consciousness, Thomas dimly realized the candles had gone out. Head throbbing, he got to
his feet and stumbled to the spiral stairs, the
ancient manuscript clutched to his chest like
a shield.

It was rumored that this pope never slept.

Indeed it was well after midnight when
Thomas Aquinas finally gained admittance
to the papal chambers, and the Holy Father
was still conferring with his advisors, Cardinal Gubbio, Cardinal Rojinsky, and Archbishop McNally.

Thomas Aquinas knew who they were, but
the cardals seemed flustered by the strange
monk's easy access to the Holy Father's private quarters. Ignoring them, Thomas approached the seated pope, kneeled, and
kissed his ring.

"What have you seen?" the pope asked,
his fragile voice barely audible.

Thomas whispered in Latin. "Your Holiness, under the sign, the eye of God, the child is born."

The Pope leaned back and murmured something in Cardinal Gubbio's ear. The rotund advisor nodded. "Send emissaries out to all the cities of the world," Cardinal Gubbio declared gravely. "She must be found."

Cardinal Rojinsky stepped nearer, his craggy face set in a righteous scowl. "She must be killed."

His judgment dangled in the quiet like a noose.

The pope's aristocratic features seemed sculpted in cold, white marble as he deliberated. He leaned back and whispered something to Cardinal Gubbio. The portly advisor nodded, then gave Cardinal Rojinsky a regretful smile.

"If we sacrifice the innocent, we do not deserve to be redeemed."

The hawk-featured prelate snorted impatiently. Cardinal Rojinsky preferred to leave matters of sin and salvation to God. "If she lives to bring about the End of Days, there will be no redemption—"

The pope raised his hand, cutting Cardinal Rojinsky off.

"The prophesy calls for faith," the pope reminded, his wispy voice trailing off. He gazed at the young monk, still kneeling at his feet. "Thomas, I charge you," he hissed, eyes

like blue suns in a white sky. "Find the girl.
Keep her from evil."

Thomas Aquinas bowed in submission as
the pope removed his silver papal cross and
slipped the sacred object over the young
monk's head.

Seething with anger and frustration, Cardinal Rojinsky glanced at the Archbishop.
They would have much to discuss later.

The falling snow shrouded Manhattan like a
lace veil. It seemed to muffle the usual blare
of night traffic. Even the ambulance sirens
arriving and departing from Our Lady of
Mercy Hospital were less strident.

Veronica York was grateful for the change.
She had been there twelve hours going
through false labor. Through her open window, Veronica could see the comet's blurred
streak above a large fuzzy moon. She felt the
cool brush of snow against her hot skin and
prayed for an end to the pain.

Just then her child decided to be born.

Veronica's husband stayed with her in the
delivery room. She squeezed his hand like a
lifeline in a raging sea. Legs up in stirrups,
she thrashed from side to side, as the agony
ebbed and swelled.

"Push," the obstetrician urged, kneeling
between her legs. "Push now . . . That's it . . .
Push."

Veronica tensed her entire body as the agony expanded and burst into an exultant flood that tore through her heaving flesh. And from somewhere beyond her pain-numbed senses she heard the triumphant cry of her newborn child.

"Congratulations—it's a girl."

Veronica opened her eyes and saw the obstetrician cradling a tiny figure in his hands, its hair matted and pink skin greased with mucus. A smiling nurse took the baby and gingerly wrapped it in a blanket. Beaming, she presented the child to Veronica.

Veronica felt a rush of emotion as she gazed at her daughter. "She's . . . She's so beautiful." Even the small, question-mark birthmark on her wrist was perfect.

Her husband's face floated into view and he kissed her gently. Both of them bent closer to their child, eyes blurred by joyful tears.

Abruptly Nurse Rand reached between them to take the swaddled child.

"I've got to take her now and clean her up."

Veronica resisted. "No, please. Not yet," she pleaded, looking at her husband.

"Hospital rules," Nurse Rand apologized. "We'll have her back before you know it."

Veronica turned to her husband. He shrugged and shook his head. As the nurse gingerly took her daughter from her arms,

Veronica felt a pang of hatred for her husband. She watched the nurse carry her child out of the room, then turned her face away . . .

Once outside, the nurse placed the child in an infant gurney and wheeled it down the corridor past the diseased and the dying. The nurse pushed the gurney into a darkened room, and locked the door behind her. She switched on the light, revealing the cadavers lying on metal slabs.

It was the hospital morgue.

The baby began to cry as the nurse wheeled the gurney past the dead bodies. A small group of people emerged from the shadows and crowded around the wailing infant.

A tall man dressed in black, wearing a Roman collar, took the child from the gurney. The others stepped back, allowing their high priest, Father Abel, to carry the screeching child to a metal table.

On the table was a large stone tablet engraved with hieroglyphics. The moment Father Abel placed the baby on the tablet, she stopped crying.

Wordlessly the group went about their ritual tasks as Father Abel intoned the prayer in Latin, invoking the dark power.

"To Him we commit your body. To Him we commit your soul . . ."

The high priest lifted the infant girl from the stone tablet, and lowered her into a surgical tray. The others removed plastic blood bags from a medical cooler.

". . . You shall open the gates to His kingdom on Earth," Father Abel droned, as the others ripped the bags and poured the blood into the tray, staining the baby's skin an obscene red.

The priest dipped his consecrated fingers into the tray and traced an oily smear across the infant's face. The baby stared at him with openmouthed amazement, but she remained quiet. Again the priest dipped into the tray and brought his bloody finger to the baby's lips.

After a moment's hesitation, the child began to suck the blood from Father Abel's finger, completing her unholy baptism . . .

Veronica hadn't spoken a word to her husband. She blamed him for not protesting when the nurse took her baby. He in turn felt guilty, but didn't really understand why. He sat stiffly, waiting for his wife to open her eyes.

Both of them turned when the door opened.

The sight of her daughter in the nurse's arms dissolved Veronica's anger. Beaming with joy, she reached out as the nurse returned her newly scrubbed baby.

"Here she is, all clean and fresh," Nurse Rand said reassuringly. "Have you thought of a name yet?"

Veronica gazed at her sleeping daughter. "Christine," she murmured, glancing at her husband. "Her name's Christine."

The nurse gave them a sweet, maternal smile.

"Happy birthday, Christine."

CHAPTER ONE

Although the sun shone brightly above the tenements that rimmed the East River like broken teeth, Jericho Cane's apartment was dark.

The sole light came from a TV screen on the floor. Flickering images rolled unseen in the gloom: faith healers babbling in the desert, politicians discussing the coming millennium as if it belonged to them, local news footage of a torched church, a documentary on signs of the Apocalypse, a potato that resembled the Virgin Mary, an image of Christ on Mars, Indian mystics whose self-inflicted wounds healed instantly, the pathetic violence of *The Jerry Springer Show* . . .

Oblivious to the electronic Tower of Babel a few feet away, Jericho Cane sat on the edge of his bed, drowning in a solitary bog of self-pity.

Jericho's living quarters reflected the

bleak, loveless quality of his life. Although he was barely forty, Jericho's apartment looked like the flat of an old man who had given up hope. Water stains darkened the bare, peeling walls, and pizza cartons and empty vodka bottles gathered dust beneath the bed frame, while Jericho sat hunched over on the soiled mattress, still dressed in a black T-shirt, military fatigues, and motorcycle boots. His sculpted, square-jawed face had the aspect of an exhausted gladiator. The faint tinkle of Christmas music drifted from a neighbor's apartment.

The only sound in the room was the metallic *click* of a gun hammer being cocked.

The gun was a Glock nine-millimeter. It was fully loaded.

And Jericho had the muzzle pressed against his skull.

The cold steel against his sweating skin abruptly pulled his mind back in time. Back to his season in hell . . .

Jericho didn't know exactly why his SEAL unit had been called into the Cambodian jungle. They were dropped in one night, black parachutes against a moonless sky.

Although a veteran of various skirmishes in Africa and Central America, Jericho hadn't been blooded in battle yet. He was young, strong . . . and stupid. He still believed the gung ho bullshit about the flag and the elite few. He still believed he was some sort of modern knight, instead of a brute hired killer.

So his nerves were bristling with anticipation as he gathered his parachute, and buried it, using his field shovel. In many ways the folding shovel was more useful than the electronic gear he carried, except for the experimental laser sight they were testing on this run. For Jericho it was love at first sight.

Jericho heard a soft whistle. He moved toward the sound and spotted a few shadowy figures in the darkness. Silently he rejoined his unit.

There were seven of them on the mission. A full bird colonel named Blake headed the unit. Their objective was to free a group of American pilots who were being held for ransom by river pirates.

A tall, wiry figure nodded a greeting as Jericho neared the group. The man's pale blue eyes had a familiar glint. Jericho was glad to see Napa had made the jump okay. The rangy blond farm boy from California had been his chief competitor during SEAL training. Lately their paths had crossed on a couple of missions.

Jericho nodded back, then took a quick head count. All seven men were down and in position, establishing a tight perimeter. They were all dressed in black tights that made them look like spandex ninjas. He crouched behind a tree, and scanned his sector. Nothing moved in the thick jungle foliage.

Jericho waited long moments, eyes peering into the darkness, before hearing a low whistle. At the sound he carefully pulled back. The others did the same.

They formed a low circle around their leader. Colonel Blake checked his watch and grunted approval. They were a few minutes ahead of schedule. Blake produced a map and a compass. "Napa," he hissed. "There's a road about a click back. Due north. Set the road to blow if anything heavier than a cow tries to cross. Move."

Napa turned and melted into the thick foliage around them. Jericho knew the Californian was an expert with mines and explosives. He had finished second to Napa in Demolition School. Jericho could handle explosives but his real specialty was face to face, hand to hand, knife and gun combat. He finished Top Gun in Assassin School.

"We rendezvous at O510, at Sector 5," Blake said tersely, tracing his finger on the map. As Jericho noted the spot, he wondered why Blake hadn't told Napa.

"Walls." Jericho looked up when he heard his nickname. Actually Napa had started it, ribbing him about the Walls of Jericho. It had stuck. "Walls and Rick will go inside with me, the rest will take position around the camp once we cross the river. Let's move."

The unit had been well-briefed, but Jericho's heart beat loudly in the dense silence. He'd been well-trained but except for a few firefights, this was his first Black Op.

Blake found a trail and they followed, each keeping a careful distance until they reached the river bank. They waited in the trees until Blake signaled. Then one by one, they ran to the river, and slipped into the dark, clammy water.

Jericho and Rick went in after Blake. The water was as warm as the steamy air and Jericho realized he was sweating even as he swam. The current was in their favor, but the automatic rifle strapped to his back started weighing him down halfway across. If it hadn't been for the new laser sight, he would have dumped it.

Gratefully he crawled up on the opposite bank and waited for Rick and Colonel Blake to emerge from the water. He scanned the area. From their pre-mission briefing he knew they were outside the camp perimeter. But he didn't know how far outside.

Then he glimpsed something moving about thirty yards away. Jericho crouched, tracking the movement through his rifle's scope. He heard a soft scrape behind him and whirled.

It was Blake. The Colonel seemed upset

that Jericho heard his approach. Jericho put a finger to his lips, then pointed. When Blake spotted the movement, he nodded and drew a finger across his throat.

Jericho hesitated, then pulled his knife from its scabbard. He moved swiftly through the sparse brush, and paused at the tree line. He had taken an angle that brought him slightly ahead of his target. As he waited, a man wearing a turban strolled into view. The man had a cigarette in one hand and an Uzi in the other. He stopped to take a long puff.

Jericho opened the man's throat with one quick slash. Blood and smoke gushed from the ragged wound as Jericho lowered the man's body to the ground. The pungent scent of blood remained with him as he hurried to re-join Colonel Blake and Rick. Immediately, insects began to swarm, attracted by the blood on his hands. Jericho was aware of a vague exhilaration. He had broken his cherry.

Suddenly a blazing yellow shaft speared the darkness across the river. A moment later a flat boom bounced across the water. Jericho heard shouting. In the dying glare of the explosion he spotted men running across a footbridge toward the flames.

"Now!" Blake grunted. "We're going in."

Blake led as they sprinted to an encampment about two hundred yards away. It was a makeshift compound of bamboo huts and tents. Many of the men housed there had crossed the footbridge to investigate the blast. But a good number had stayed, and remained on full alert, prowling nervously, weapons twitching at every sound.

Rick took out the first guard with a classic ploy. He tossed his knife on the ground. When the guard bent to pick it up, Rick pounced, clubbing the man with his rifle. A moment later the man was dead. Rick gave them the high sign.

Blake and Jericho took out the next two guards with the same textbook precision. They each clamped their hands over their victims' mouths to muffle any outcries and killed them with a single knife slash. They exchanged a mad glance, then trotted through the compound.

Blake seemed to know where he was going. He stopped outside a bamboo hut and motioned to Rick and Jericho. They stopped and looked at him. Blake lifted his hand and made a mock pistol with his thumb and forefinger. For emphasis he wagged his finger. Jericho got the message. He slid his knife into its scabbard and gripped his rifle.

The entrance to the bamboo hut was narrow, allowing only one man at a time. Blake pointed at Jericho. Without hesitation Jericho moved to the door and stepped inside.

Four men were seated at a wooden table,

drinking and playing cards. All sat with their weapons on their laps. The moment Jericho entered they reached down. Jericho's rifle chattered like a sewing machine, stitching bullets across the table. Cards and shattered glass flew into the air as the men dove to the floor. A bullet *snapped* past his ear and Jericho realized they were firing at him. Then he saw two of the men jerking like puppets as his gunfire filled the room. A moment later it was silent.

A strange wailing floated up in the smoky quiet. At first Jericho thought it came from one of the men scattered across the bloody floor. But then he saw Colonel Blake push the wooden table aside and reach down. Blake pulled open a large trapdoor made of steel bars. When Jericho moved closer, he saw it was the door to a prison pit. Trapped below were the four American pilots.

They sure don't look like military pilots, Jericho thought, noting the tattoos and earrings sported by a couple of them. Judging from their hefty condition, they hadn't been imprisoned long. He watched as Colonel Blake and Rick pulled the pilots out of the pit. The hairs on his neck prickled and he heard a soft sound behind him. Jericho whirled in time to see a turbaned figure in black pajamas step into the room and start shooting.

The intruder managed about three rounds

before Jericho brought him down with a short burst. Blake gave Jericho a curt nod of approval, then pointed at the door, saying "Move out!"

Before leaving, Rick tossed a grenade into the hut. The flaming blast helped light their escape, but it also made them easier targets. As they ran toward jungle cover, a sudden shower of bullets spattered around them. One pilot suffered a flesh wound, forcing them to drop and find cover.

The gunfire was coming from a half-dozen men on the other side of the footbridge. The men kept advancing over the ridge, guns spitting deadly fire.

"Stay down!" Blake yelled.

Jericho switched on the laser sight. The thin red beam cut through smoke and shadow and pinned the lead attacker squarely in the chest. Jericho brought him down with one shot. He kept firing and watched the rest scramble away from the dancing light. He saw one straggler go down, hit in the leg.

"Walls—cover us and blow the bridge!" Blake yelled. "Everybody move out."

Jericho fired a long burst as the others ran into the jungle and vanished. Then he jacked a fresh clip in his rifle and slowly advanced to the bridge. Crouching behind one of the thick wooden stakes that anchored the bridge, Jericho peered across.

One dead pirate lay in the middle of the narrow bridge. Another pirate lay further beyond. Jericho saw him moving, as if trying to crawl to the other side. He also saw two men creeping toward their wounded comrade.

Suddenly Jericho remembered Napa. If he blew the bridge, Napa wouldn't be able to keep their rendezvous with the helicopter.

The pencil-thin laser beamed through the darkness and found both would-be rescuers. Jericho took them out with two quick shots, then sprinted across the bridge, rifle blazing. As he ran past the wounded man a loud *crack* split the darkness. Before the man could get off another shot, Jericho turned and blew his chest open.

Jericho kept firing short bursts as he ran, until he reached the other side. Once across he dove to the ground and rolled, expecting a hail of gunfire.

It never came. The remaining pirates had decided to cut their losses and retreat. Recklessly Jericho charged towards the flickering glow that marked Napa's road kill.

Napa had set his charges well. The burning remains of a Mercedes bus lit up both sides of the road. The bomb had split the vehicle neatly in two, spilling its human contents like so many egg yolks.

Jericho moved off the road and searched the area for a sign of Napa. The rangy SEAL would have left behind some equipment when he bugged out. Then Jericho spotted him. The young Californian was lying at the base of a tree. When Jericho neared, he saw the knife handle protruding from Napa's bloody sternum. There was something familiar about the knife. Stunned, Jericho realized it was an official issue SEAL combat knife.

Napa had been assassinated by one of his own.

Abruptly Napa's eyes opened. When he saw Jericho he tried to speak. "Easy," Jericho grunted reaching for his medical kit. "Bus . . ." Napa groaned.

"It's okay," Jericho whispered. He jabbed the morphine needle into Napa's arm. Immediately Napa's features relaxed and he managed a smile of thanks as the pain ebbed.

"Bus . . ." Napa repeated. "Pree . . ." Then he died.

Emotions churning, Jericho stood up and carefully approached the burning bus. The front had blown forward, and the rear section twisted sideways. As Jericho glanced at the victims splayed across the road he froze, paralyzed by cold shock.

The bus had been carrying priests and nuns.

Through his confusion, Jericho's survival instincts took over. He checked his watch. Less than ten minutes to get to the chopper.

Figure it out on the way home, Jericho told himself. *This is no place to play detective.*

Jericho retraced his path to the footbridge and sprinted across. This time he encountered no resistance. In the light of the single burning hut, he could see the compound was deserted. To cover himself, Jericho set two grenades on slow fuse on either side of the bridge. They exploded as he ran into the jungle. He didn't bother to turn around and admire his work.

As it was, the chopper had already loaded all survivors and was lifting off four minutes ahead of schedule when Jericho reached the rendezvous point. Instinctively he knew Colonel Blake wouldn't hold the chopper—and he was right.

Even as he dashed across the clearing, Jericho could see Blake staring at him from the open door, but the chopper kept lifting higher off the ground. Jericho dropped his rifle and raced toward the departing craft, legs pumping wildly. At the last moment he dove and grabbed the skids. For a dizzying second he swung in mid-air as the chopper lifted higher. Then a strong hand clamped his wrist. Jericho looked up. It was Blake.

For a moment, just before pulling him inside, Blake's gray eyes searched Jericho's face as if judging whether to drop him or take him aboard. Then he heaved Jericho through the door.

It was clear he wasn't welcome. Jericho could feel the hostility from the pilots he had just rescued. Jericho looked at Blake and grinned. "Thanks, Colonel. Mission accomplished."

Blake didn't say anything.

Jericho looked around. "Where's Napa?"

Blake shrugged. "Didn't make it." Jericho dropped his head, but he sensed that Blake was still suspicious.

"Why so long to blow the bridge?" Blake's quiet question cut like a razor. Jericho lifted his hands. They were stained with Napa's blood. "Two of them jumped me." He glanced around. All four pilots were staring at him.

Blake gave him a small smile. "They picked the wrong SEAL." After that everyone seemed more relaxed but Jericho stayed alert all the way back to base camp. People often fell out of choppers in Cambodia.

Although the Vietnam war was long over, the CIA still maintained a secret airstrip on the Cambodian border. Jericho's unit was given temporary quarters while they waited for transport back to Hawaii. Seven of them had gone on the mission, six had returned. *And one of them killed Napa*, Jericho reflected, as he lay on his bunk. He watched the others through slitted eyes, wondering who it was. Rick was with him so it had to be someone on Team B. *But why?*

That night, while waiting to board the
transport, Jericho noticed a number of crates
being loaded. He walked over to the cargo
area and bummed a cigarette from the guard.
The guard grudgingly gave him a smoke.
Jericho paused to light the cigarette and in
that moment managed to get a clear look at
the nearest crate. Stenciled on the side was
the code GR1097 NapaCa. GR—*Graves Reg-
istration.* Jericho moved back to the passen-
ger stairs. He knew better than to ask
questions.

When they landed in Honolulu, Colonel
Blake gave everyone seven days of R&R. Jericho checked into a hotel, then went back to
the military airport where their transport
had landed. He made sure he got there at
chow time.

"They lost my duffel bag on the flight,"
Jericho told the guards at the cargo area. "I
was told they would have it back here."
Since his ID and paperwork checked out, the
guards let him go back and take a look while
they ate their meal. Jericho found the crates
and hurridly opened the one marked
NapaCa. Inside was a body bag packed in
ice. Jericho unzipped the bag and saw
Napa's boyish face. He looked back at the
entrance gate and saw the guards were still
eating dinner. Moving to another crate, he
quickly pried it open.

It was another body bag. When Jericho unzipped it, he found it was a priest. *One of the priests on the bus*, Jericho thought. But as he started to close the bag, something blocked the zipper. Jericho shifted the body and stopped. For a long moment he gaped at the neat plastic bag beneath the priest's shoulder. Without hesitation Jericho cut a small slit in the plastic. The knife tip came out covered with white powder. The bitter taste confirmed what he already knew. Heroin.

He hastily replaced the lid and glanced at the entrance gate. The guards were laughing about something. Jericho rechecked Napa's crate and found the same thing—plastic bags of heroin beneath his friend's body.

"Hey, you find anything yet?" Jericho saw a guard walking over and closed the crate. He walked back to meet the guard. "Not here. Where's this shipment headed?"

The guard snorted. "This load is all stiffs. And they're headed to L.A. tonight."

"Stiffs?" Jericho repeated, pretending surprise.

"Yeah. Didn't you hear? Communists in Cambodia blew up a busload of missionaries. It was all over the news."

"Fucking brass never tell us anything."

The guard gave him a sympathetic nod.

"Look," Jericho said. "Can you tell me where that load is going in L.A.? Maybe they sent my bag ahead."

The guard shrugged and checked the manifest. "LAX, Hangar 55. That's all I've got."

It was all Jericho needed. He took the next flight out and when the military transport landed, he was waiting in Hangar 55. Jericho had taken a position behind a forklift and when the hangar doors swung open, he had a clear view.

A truck stacked with the crated bodies rolled inside. Jericho watched as the crates were unloaded and the truck rolled out. Within minutes, a black car entered the hangar. Two men got out and closed the hangar door behind them.

One of the men was Colonel Blake. Jericho recognized the other one as the new man in their unit, Cronin. And Cronin had been on Team B. *The bastard killed Napa*, Jericho thought, his jaw knotted with rage. *This whole op was about drugs and money*.

Jericho checked his weapons. He had a .45, a knife, and a grenade; all of which had made it past a civilian baggage check. He watched as Blake and Cronin opened the crates and loaded the plastic bags into the trunk of their car.

A loud knock broke the quiet. Blake opened the door and a second black car entered the hangar. Three men got out of the car. Two were big and burly, wearing black suits and ponytails. The driver looked like a gang kid. He had tattoos on both hands and a long scar along one cheek.

One of the ponytails carried an attaché case. The other carried an Uzi. The driver was unarmed.

Blake showed the man the contents of the trunk. One of the ponytails took a glass vial from his pocket and tested the heroin. The whole process took less than five minutes. Finally the ponytail shut the trunk and handed Blake the attaché case. Blake handed him the car keys. Then Blake and Cronin went to the other car and started the motor. It was a simple car switch. In a few moments they'd be gone.

But as Blake slowly rolled the car out of the hangar, a wheezing vehicle lurched out of the shadows and blocked his path. High in the driver's chair of the forklift, Jericho speared the grill with the steel forks and lifted the car off the ground. He could see Blake and Cronin staring at him with a mixture of disbelief and fury.

A bullet *pinged* off the side of the forklift. Jericho glimpsed a ponytail edging around Blake's car and fired twice. As one ponytail fell, the other came running. He fired wildly with his Uzi, but Jericho had dropped behind the forklift.

The ponytail and Cronin each took one side of the forklift and closed fast, guns blazing. But Jericho wasn't there.

Both gunmen stood confused, scanning both sides of the hangar. Abruptly, the air above them exploded, but they never heard it. Jericho shot them both from the top of a steel container.

When Jericho dropped to the floor, his eyes were on one man. Blake was running toward the other car. The young gangbanger was behind the wheel and he was backing the car away from the gunfire. Jericho sprinted after Blake, his blood pounding with a primal need for revenge. Blake was slowed by the leather case clutched in his fist.

The car stopped backing away, and Jericho could see the driver assessing the situation. The driver opted to scoop up Blake on his way to the exit. He leaned over, opened the car door, and stepped on the accelerator. The loud screech pierced the shuffling quiet.

Blake charged hard as the car roared near. When it squealed to a stop, he dove for the open door. But suddenly it slammed shut— as Jericho's bullet smacked the door! The bullet went through, wounding the driver, who opened his door and half-fell to the ground.

Rolling aside, Blake came up shooting. His first two bullets missed but the third grazed Jericho's arm. Jericho didn't seem to notice. He kept coming, his .45 blasting. His first shot grazed Blake's neck, cutting a bright red scar.

Both men stood their ground, guns extended like French duelists, and eyes glassy with primitive battle rage. Jericho's next shot hit Blake's shoulder and he fell back. But when Jericho walked closer, aimed at Blake's head, and pulled the trigger—it *clicked*. Empty.

Jericho numbly watched Blake lift his own .45 and point its ugly snout directly at his groin. Smiling, Blake pulled the trigger. *Click!* Empty. It was Jericho's turned to smile. *Fitting,* he thought. *Since Napa was killed by a SEAL knife.*

Blake was tough but no match for Jericho's wrath. Jericho pounced like a big cat, drawing his knife as he dropped down on his wounded prey. The struggle was brief, and final. When Jericho stood up, Blake was dead. Jericho hopped back when he pulled his knife from Blake's heart, avoiding the bloody geyser that spurted from the gash in his chest.

A faint shuffle alerted his senses. Jericho whirled and saw the young driver limping— near a fallen Uzi. The driver glanced at it and froze. The Uzi was only a few feet away. The young driver could easily snatch it up and fire. Jericho could see the driver's scarred face twitching as he weighed his odds, one arm poised in the air like a tattooed lady justice.

Jericho locked on the driver's eyes. Slowly he lifted the knife and licked the blood. Then he slowly advanced on the horrified gang-banger. That's all it took to convince the young driver to abandon the weapon and run for cover. Scuttling like a crab on meth-adrine, he vanished between the stacks of crates and containers.

Jericho decided to let him live. He had accomplished his mission. Retrieving Blake's fallen attaché case, Jericho got into the car. He sped out of the hangar to the spot where he had parked his rented Corvette. Before he drove off with the case, Jericho set a grenade on a ten-minute fuse and dropped it into the heroin-filled trunk. As he drove off toward a nearby freeway, Jericho heard the faint wail of police sirens. He never did hear the grenade blast Blake's heroin to black ash.

The leather case contained a half million dollars.

Jericho gave most of it to Napa's young widow. He kept some to set himself up in New York after he resigned from the SEALS. The Navy offered to make him an officer and a gentleman if he re-upped, but Jericho no longer believed in the honor of war.

Four years later he was a highly paid security expert, with a family—his wife Emily and his daughter Amy.

Four years. That's how long it took for the gangbanger with the scarred face to track him down. Jericho was away on assignment. His wife asked him to stay home for a while but Jericho's best client, a senator, needed a personal escort for a Caribbean cruise. A fat fee and a tan, what could be better? After that he planned to take Emily and Amy on vacation.

It never came. When Jericho returned, he had no family.

Intruders had bypassed his own security system and broken into his home. They took their time with Emily and Amy before they murdered them. The graphic police report continued to haunt Jericho.

The killers left behind a knife—special issue SEAL.

What Jericho hadn't known was that the tattooed gangbanger was actually Mr. Big. It was his money—and his heroin—that Jericho blew away. The gangbanger knew nothing about Napa, and his only code of honor was revenge.

A month after the funeral Jericho took a leave of absence. He flew to L.A. and rented a sunny apartment in Santa Monica. Then he started hanging around East L.A., scoring small amounts of dope. Eventually he became considered a regular. He was even rousted by the police a few times. Soon he had a name—Mr. Earl.

One day he saw Mr. Earl, all decked out in shades and leather, cruising through the 'hood in his cherry red Caddy. It was the same man Jericho had let live four years before.

It hadn't been easy. First he had to kill two large, highly motivated bodyguards. Then he had to keep himself from killing his enemy too soon. Mr. Earl had taken his time with his family, and Jericho wanted to return the favor.

Jericho left Mr. Earl's head on his red caddy like a hood ornament.

Since then Jericho had been on a ten-year binge: women, booze, drugs. But he couldn't forget and he wouldn't die. *God knows I tried hard enough*, Jericho reflected grimly.

In his work as a security specialist, he always volunteered for the dangerous assignments. Unfortunately his instincts and skills always pulled him through.

Not today, Jericho thought. *Today is the first day of my death.*

He took a deep breath, steadied the gun against his skull and tightened his finger around the trigger . . .

CHAPTER TWO

The muscles cording his forearm trembled as his finger caressed the trigger. Jericho's muscular chest heaved beneath his sweat-soaked T-shirt. His jaw knotted and he squeezed.

Bam! Bam! Bam!

The loud, insistent knocking at the door stilled his finger on the trigger—but not his decision to end it all. Sweat glistened on his face as he tried to find the strength to put a bullet in his brain.

There was a jingling of keys. A slash of light slid across the floor when the door opened, then receded as the door closed.

"Honey . . . I'm home."

A dark-haired man holding something in his fist came into the room. Jericho dimly recognized Chicago, his partner and best friend.

"C'mon, Jer, we're gonna be late."

Reluctantly Jericho released the hammer

and put the gun aside. "I was just pulling myself together."

Chicago squinted through the gloom. "That might take a lot of pulling." He moved to the window and opened the venetian blinds. The sudden glare revealed the apartment in all its squalid sadness. One table, one, chair, no pictures, no Christmas cards, and an ever-babbling TV on the floor. Jericho himself looked as pale as an eggshell about to crumble. His muscular frame seemed hollow, and his deep-set cobalt eyes were as empty as the Stoli bottle on his night table.

"You're looking real sharp."

Jericho fell back on the bed. "Thank you."

"You're welcome. You've got five minutes to change." Chicago rattled the paper bag in his fist. "We're gonna be late."

Jericho groaned and sat up. Chicago reached into the paper bag and took out a quart container of coffee. "There's enough caffeine in here to kill an elephant. It should get you started."

Wincing, Jericho took the container, then swung his feet to the floor. He awkwardly pushed himself erect, thick-muscled limbs stiff and aching.

"What's today?" Jericho grunted, brushing past on his way to the kitchen.

Chicago followed, but stayed well back when Jericho opened the refrigerator. His

partner hated to throw good food—or bad—
away. Eventually things took on a life of
their own and moved to a better place.

"Today we got Transport," Chicago said,
flashing a glossy black file.

Jericho pulled out some leftover fried rice
and pizza, and dumped them into a blender.
"Anyone special?"

"Just some Wall Street scumbag."

"Why does he need all that protection?"

"He fucked over some people that don't
like being fucked over."

Jericho opened a bottle of Pepto-Bismol. "I
like scumbags—they pay better."

Chicago watched with morbid fascination
as his partner poured some Pepto into the
blender with the leftovers—and added the
steaming coffee.

Jericho turned and gave him a wicked
grin. "They say breakfast is the most important meal of the day."

Then he pushed BLEND.

Despite the snowfall the night before, it
turned out to be one of those crisp, clear days
when everyone congratulated themselves on
living in New York. Kids were tossing fris-
bees in the Sheep Meadow, adults were
promenading along Madison Avenue, and
tourists were gawking at the tree in Rockefel-
ler Center, still festooned with holiday glitter.

A few feet from Tiffany's elegant windows, a homeless albino prayed to a steaming manhole. His pink eyes rolled up as a shadow swept across the street.

A black helicopter circled low as police sirens whined in the distance. The white-skinned derelict turned back to his prayers, bowing to the gray puffs of steam bubbling from the manhole. He didn't even look up when the wailing motorcade snaked past.

The black helicopter swooped down just ahead of the motorcade, dipping low enough for curious pedestrians to read the STRIKER PRIVATE SECURITY logo emblazoned on its side. The helicopter pilot, Sam Yates, calmly surveyed both sides of the street, then switched on his mike. "This is Sky Two. Rooftops one-two-five through one-three-six are clear. Repeat clear. Proceed with client."

Seated inside a black Infiniti sedan trailing the client's limo, Jericho Cane lifted his shirt cuff to his lips. "Roger Sky Two. Follow Alpha is on approach," he droned into the small microphone clipped to his cuff. "ETA two minutes."

At the wheel, Chicago glanced at his partner. Dressed in a crisp new shirt and sharply pressed suit, Jericho looked like the cool, highly skilled professional he was. *A far cry from the vodka-soaked wreck I roused two hours ago*, Chicago noted with grudging admiration. The Big Cat had remarkable recuperative powers.

As Chicago drove, Jericho's deep-set blue eyes constantly scanned the street—windows, roofs, pedestrians, vendors—everything. His mind and body were on hyper-alert. At the same time Jericho methodically checked his twin Glock nine-millimeter pistols before slipping them into the quick-draw holsters strapped to both his wrists. The Glocks were holstered butt down—so Jericho could draw them both by bringing his hands together. Chicago had seen him do it. Or more precisely, he'd seen two Glock nines leap into the Big Cat's hands out of nowhere.

The client's limo was nearing its destination. Jericho kept his eyes on the street but he was uncomfortably aware of his partner. They'd worked, played, and fought together long enough to develop a silent form of communication. And Jericho knew Chicago was worried about him. *Hell, he's got good cause*, Jericho brooded. *I'm worried myself.*

Jericho's thoughts were cut short by the red flare of the limo's brake lights ahead. As Chicago slowed down, Jericho opened the door and hit the ground running. "We're exposed," Jericho drawled into his cuff mike, alerting the helicopter. Chicago left the sedan and covered Jericho's back as he trotted to the limo and opened the door. The limo driver, another Striker Security guard, got out and covered the street.

When the client emerged, he was met by four executives who'd been waiting for their honored guest in front of the bank building. Jericho stood to one side as the executives bowed and scraped, his intense gaze assessing each pedestrian and passing vehicle.

A metallic glint caught the corner of his eye and he glanced up. As the client walked toward the bank, Jericho scanned the old-fashioned brick building next door. Nothing.

Then he spotted it again—near the top of the fire escape, like sunlight glinting off a mirror. Most would have dismissed it. Instantly, Jericho sprang into combat mode.

"Sky Two—fire escape southwest sector," he called hoarsely.

Sam Yates tilted the hovering 'copter and peered down at the brick building next to the bank. Both its roof and grilled fire escape were deserted. "Fire escape negative . . ."

"You're wrong!" Jericho barked. "*Shooter*! Evac! Evac!"

As Chicago and the driver fumbled for their weapons, Jericho grabbed the client by the shoulders, spun him around, and tossed him headfirst into the limo. A gunshot cracked, adding to the confusion. Jericho looked back. Suddenly his tailored suit jacket exploded twice in quick sequence as hollow-point bullets blasted him squarely in the chest. Falling, Jericho slammed the limo door shut.

The limousine took off screeching, knocking Jericho aside as it fled the scene. Chicago raced toward Jericho's crumpled body while uniformed security guards rushed out of the bank. Amidst the frantic chaos, Chicago felt strangely calm. Jericho lay motionless on the cement. Chicago knelt beside him and fingered the gaping bullet holes in his shirt.

"Call NYPD and get an ambulance," Chicago yelled into the tiny microphone wired to his cuff. He looked down, rough features tight with concern.

"C'mon . . . Get up, you pussy," Chicago muttered urgently.

Jericho stirred. His eyelids fluttered open and he regarded Chicago accusingly. "I thought it was your turn to get shot."

Chicago slowly exhaled. "No. I got it last time." He reached out and helped Jericho to his feet. Jericho ripped open the front of his shirt. Both bullets were imbedded in his Kevlar vest.

"What a morning. I should have stayed in bed."

Chicago squinted up at the brick building. "Too bad you wore the vest, man. You could have been out of your misery."

The barb struck home. Ignoring the pain stabbing his torso, Jericho followed Chicago's gaze. "Where's the shooter?"

"Heading for the roof."

"Then why are we down here?"

Before Jericho finished the question, Chicago was calling the helicopter. Immediately the craft descended, but it couldn't land. Stalled traffic clogged the entire block.

Jericho didn't hesitate. Nimbly he mounted the trunk of the nearest car, then leaped onto the vinyl roof. With Chicago close behind, Jericho raced across the jammed car rooftops until he reached the hovering copter. Both men stepped onto the skid and scrambled on board. Immediately the helicopter lifted off.

"There," Chicago said, pointing at a white-haired figure climbing the fire escape of the brick building. They watched him through the side window.

The fleeing shooter climbed onto the roof and took a position behind a stack of crates. As the helicopter approached, he fired. The helicopter's side window shattered in a roar of flying glass and rushing wind. The craft lurched, then steadied. Chicago and Jericho drew their sidearms, leaned out the broken window, and began pumping rounds at the shooter.

"Down!" Jericho shouted. "Get us closer!"

Struggling with the controls, Sam Yates circled lower, giving them a better angle. The shooter fired wildly from behind the crates. Jericho answered with seven quick shots that blasted the crates apart and flushed him into the open. The shooter started to run, then whirled, rifle aimed directly at the cockpit—but the shot never came. They saw the shooter toss the rifle aside, obviously out of ammo.

"It's over," Chicago said. He spoke too soon.

The shooter ran back and forth, looking for an escape route.

"Set us down!" Jericho yelled. "Hurry!"

Sam Yates shook his head. "There's too much crap on that roof—we'd break the main rotor off."

Jericho turned to Chicago. "Snap me in!" He glared at the pilot. "Stay with him."

Skillfully Sam Yates descended in front of the shooter, cutting him off. The shooter paused, then started backing away as Jericho hit the safety brake on the winch and started trailing rope out of the open door.

The shooter weighed his options. Suddenly he turned and began sprinting for the edge of the building.

Chicago leaned out the window. "He's gonna take a dive!"

"Not before I kick his ass," Jericho

grunted. He pulled the rope taut and edged out of the copter. "ON HIM!"

Eyes on their quarry, Sam Yates bounced the helicopter in a soft arc that dropped them beside the shooter. He kept the craft steady as the shooter charged headlong toward the edge. Dangling from the rope, skimming the roof, Jericho reached out for the shooter, less than a foot away. The man continued for the edge, arms and legs pumping crazily. Jericho reached for him, but missed.

Suddenly the roof fell away and a forty-story drop yawned beneath him. At that moment the shooter jumped. Reflexively Jericho swiped at him, and his fingers clutched something. A sudden yank almost tore it from his hands but he squeezed tight. Looking down he saw the shooter dangling beneath him, legs kicking.

Somehow he'd grabbed the shooter's coat. Shoulder straining, he lifted the shooter with one hand and squeezed the rappel brake with the other, pulling them up. They swung onto the skid and the helicopter rose in the air, turning back toward the roof. Without warning the shooter kicked at Jericho's crotch, then yanked a small handgun from his ankle holster. Jericho's eyes went wide as the muzzle came up to his face. "Not today, baby," he grunted, snatching the shooter's wrist.

Unfortunately he let go of the rappel brake.

Both men tumbled off the skid and began a sickening free fall to the concrete forty stories below. The rope whistled through the rappelling harness as the ground rose up to meet them. Frantically Jericho swatted the pistol away and grabbed the brake with one hand, while holding the shooter with the other. Jericho squeezed the brake and the rope screeched to a jolting halt. For a moment the shooter hovered forty feet above the street, arms spread like a skydiver. Then the coat slipped out of Jericho's hand.

Jericho watched the shooter hit the side of a sloping glass building, ten feet below. The canopy shattered and the shooter fell into a newstand, landing in a pile of magazines and candy bars.

He banged the side of the copter. "Take me down!"

"I can't land in the middle of a crowded street!" the pilot croaked, starting his descent. The shooter saw them coming and painfully pushed himself up.

"Fuck it," Chicago shouted at Jericho. "It's a police problem now."

"Bullshit," Jericho snapped. "He wanted me, he gets me." He stepped onto the skid and watched the shooter lurch toward a subway station.

Aware of the dangling rope, Sam Yates dropped as low as he dared, but too high for anyone to jump. Jericho couldn't wait. He jumped anyway. He hit the broad roof of a passing bus and rolled off as it passed the subway station. Jericho scrambled down the metal stairs in time to see the shooter duck into a dark passage marked EMERGENCY EXIT.

Without hesitation Jericho followed. His heart and lungs heaved against his bruised ribs, his shoulder ached, and one knee had twisted when he jumped. But he charged after the shooter with relentless intensity, ignoring everything except his quarry.

The dark passage opened onto a wide, dimly lit tunnel, steam vented from dirty pools of water between the rusty tracks. Jericho heard something and saw rats scurry toward him. A moment later the sharp *clap* of gun shots sent him diving for cover.

Jericho rolled and fired blindly, bullets whining into the darkness. A thick silence blanketed the tunnel. Jericho got up and stepped into the open. He paused a moment until his eyes adjusted to the gloom. Then, moving as stealthily as a cat, he crept down the tunnel. He heard the distant rumble of an approaching train. The tracks rattled and the overhead lights flickered as the rumble grew louder. It felt as if a train were rushing past on the other side of the wall. Except there was no train.

In the strobing light Jericho glimpsed the shooter. The white-haired man stepped out into the open and raised his hand. "Heed me, Jericho," he bellowed above the roar. "The thousand years are over. The Dark Angel is loosed from his prison. There's nothing you can do to stop him."

Jericho's skin prickled at the sound of his name. *How does the crazy bastard know who I am?* he wondered. Without waiting for an answer he stepped out and fixed the shooter in his sights.

"Get down on the ground," he rasped breathlessly. "Hands behind your head! Now!"

The shooter ignored him. "You don't know what you've done!"

As he came closer, Jericho could see the messianic fervor glazing the shooter's wide gray eyes. In the strobing light he resembled a gaunt Biblical prophet, long hair swept by a divine storm.

Jericho stared down the barrel of his gun. "Get down—or I'm going to put you down."

The shooter stalked closer. "You don't know what you've done!"

Jericho changed the angle of his shot and fired. The shooter screamed. At the same time, the lights blinked off. In that long moment of total blackness Jericho felt an icy dread slither across his belly. He shivered, dimly aware the train was gone.

CHAPTER THREE

When the lights blinked on, Jericho cautiously approached the shooter. He was mildly surprised to see he had stitched two bullets in the shooter's leg. He was even more surprised when he opened the man's shirt to help him breathe.

The shooter was wearing a priest's collar under his shirt.

Weird, Jericho thought, going through his pockets. He found a wallet. Empty. He searched the other pockets and found a matchbook. The name on the cover read Mullin's Bar.

He heard footsteps and labored breathing behind him. Chicago had finally caught up. Jericho showed him the matchbook.

"This guy can't be all bad . . . At least he drinks."

Chicago gave him an exasperated look as

Jericho pocketed the matchbook. "Maybe the cops would like to have that. I think it's called evidence."

"I want a head start. There's no reason to make it easy for them."

Easy for who? Chicago wondered. But before he could ask, the cops started to arrive, flashlights bobbing in the gloom.

In a way, Jericho turned out to be right. The police swarmed over the tracks, trampling any other evidence that might have fallen. Jericho stood to the side while the paramedics loaded the wounded man onto a stretcher. The shooter rolled his eyes and spotted Jericho. He tried to speak, but only guttural barks came from his lips.

Jericho moved away from the bustling officers, to where Chicago stood, smoking a cigarette. Jericho took out the matchbook and studied it intently. He looked at Chicago and shrugged. "All the best clues come from the perp's pocket."

Chicago nudged him and jerked his head. Jericho looked up and saw Detective Marge Francis approaching. She was frowning at some papers in her hand and shaking her head.

"Marge don't look too happy with our statements," Chicago warned.

"Should have killed him," Jericho said sadly. "Less paperwork."

Detective Marge Francis was an attractive redhead on the good side of forty. But police work aged one quickly. There were blue shadows around her eyes and tension webbed her creamy skin. As she approached the two men she unconsciously brushed back her hair. She had worked with Jericho when he was on the force, and she still hadn't gotten over him.

"Detective," Chicago greeted.

"Bobby," she said briskly. "Hey, Jer, been a while."

Jericho gave her a tight smile. "Yeah. How are you, Marge?"

"Can't complain. You?"

He shrugged. As usual, he gave the police nothing.

"Nice day to jump out of a helicopter?" she suggested.

"Just doing my job."

"Yeah, well, listen . . . there's something I gotta ask you."

Her casual tone alerted Jericho.

"What's that?" he said guardedly.

"You, uh, still drinking?"

"What's *that* got to do with anything?" Chicago said indignantly.

"I was just reading his statement." She looked at Jericho. "You said the guy spoke to you."

"That's right. So what?"

"Jer—the guy has no tongue."

Confusion and disbelief collided in his brain. He gaped at her, unable to comprehend.

Marge gave him a maternal smile and patted his shoulder. "Listen, what do you say I leave out that detail right now?" she whispered. "No big deal, right?"

Jericho stiffened. She was patronizing him, like some errant outpatient.

"You saying I imagined it?"

Marge threw up her hands and walked away. "No, Jer . . ." she intoned with exaggerated patience. ". . . I'm just saying."

Jericho's confusion spilled over into anger. "I saved a life today," he called after her. "What did you do?"

"Let it go, man. Let it go," Chicago muttered.

Jericho fingered the matchbook he'd taken from the shooter.

"I know what I heard," he said under his breath.

Mullin's Bar was tucked away between Little India on East 6th Street, and the Ukrainian neighborhood on 7th. It had a jukebox that still took quarters, a cigarette machine that stocked unfiltered brands, and the tin walls were dotted with flyspecked photos of bygone athletes.

Jericho liked the place immediately. Chicago yearned for something more upscale like Odeon. But this was business.

After a brief conversation with the bartender, Jericho had what he wanted. On the way outside, he explained his deductive technique to Chicago.

"A drunk hangs out at a neighborhood bar . . . he passes out enough times . . . and people know where he lives from carrying him home," Jericho said with grim humor. "This is something I know."

"It's nice to be an expert on something," Chicago agreed.

"It took years of research."

Chicago wasn't laughing. He knew his partner was hanging by a thread, despite his heroics that morning. If anything, Jericho was too reckless for a professional. *Maybe too reckless for a partner*, Chicago speculated morosely. *Nothing worse on this job than a death wish.*

Chicago shook off his doubts. When push came to shove there was nobody he'd rather have at his back. Bottom line—Jericho was the best.

The Big Cat had been the best in the SEALs. The best on the police SWAT team. And now he was the number-one security expert in the country. *Maybe the planet*, Chicago speculated.

The address the bartender gave them turned out to be an abandoned building. Chicago was ready to call it a day, but Jericho switched on his flashlight and went inside. After checking the deserted street, Chicago followed.

He wished he hadn't as soon as he entered. The stink of dank water and human refuse filled the narrow hall. The cracked plaster walls revealed a rusted web of leaking pipes. Roaches and rats scurried away from their flashlight beams.

Jericho motioned Chicago toward the stairs. Coming closer, Chicago saw a faint light glowing from behind a door above them. They both beamed their flashlights up the stairway.

Strange symbols and shapes were painted on the stairs and walls.

"Wanna bet it's rent controlled?" Chicago muttered.

Ignoring him, Jericho mounted the stairs. They were made of stone and mortar that crumbled under their feet, but the big man didn't make a sound.

They slowly edged down the hallway, toward the dim glow. When they reached the doorway, Jericho motioned Chicago, who drew his gun and crouched in a cover position. Jericho went inside first, low and fast.

A moment later Chicago stepped into hell's own crash pad.

The windows were painted black, and the floors and rickety furniture were swamped with moldy food, broken objects, and grotesque images. Their sweeping flashlights revealed a rotting mattress in one corner. Roaches rustled away from the light.

Chicago was also anxious to leave. "Couldn't this be considered breaking and entering?" he whispered.

"We haven't broken anything yet." Jericho struck a match and lit several candles on an old-fashioned writing desk. Their pale illumination settled across the room, revealing a graveyard of mutilated, deformed religious icons.

Disfigured Madonnas, mutilated crosses, and broken statues of angels and saints were strewn across the floor in some sort of perverse order. Chicago noticed a shiny red triangle smeared on the floor. It was sticky to the touch. Chicago's belly turned over.

"I don't think this is paint," he hissed.

Jericho scowled and turned his attention to the walls. They were covered with drawings, all done by the same spidery hand. Pictures of angels and demons in gory combat over broken human bones and screaming skulls, religious icons and symbols, and wildly scrawled graffiti.

"Real art buff," Chicago murmured, examining a rendering of Hades that featured tortured souls impaled on burning spikes. "I was going to do my living room just like this, but I thought it was . . . too busy."

Jericho bent closer to read the scrawls on the wall. " 'I have seen the earth laid to waste,' he recited slowly. 'I have seen the horror to come. Is it a sin to wish you were never born . . . ?' "

The question hovered in the stifling quiet.

Around the scrawl, were the numbers 20–7, written over and over, like a numerical frame. "Twenty . . . seven . . ." Jericho muttered.

"Football score?" Chicago suggested. The hollow attempt at humor failed to ease his looming sense of danger.

A large silver cross on the wall drew Jericho's curiosity. The object was vaguely familiar. The ornately carved cross looked like a museum piece. Except for the fact that it had been hacked and twisted, and a small spike was hammered through its center. But Jericho recognized the object from a previous assignment at the Vatican. It was a papal cross, worn only by the pope.

Just beneath the cross was a small, dark hole. Perhaps the hammer that spiked the cross had missed a blow or two. Jericho shone his light inside.

There was something in there.

Chicago winced as Jericho rolled up his sleeve and pushed his hand past the cobwebs and roaches. When he pulled out his hand, he was holding a pickle jar. A pickle was still floating inside. Except it wasn't a pickle.

"What the hell is that?" Chicago asked in a hushed voice.

"His tongue."

Chicago was sorry he had asked. He gaped at the blackened lump of flesh floating inside the jar.

Jericho picked up a pair of long shears from a nearby stool. "He must have cut it off himself," he mused, regarding the jar like Yorick's skull.

"Why would anyone cut out their own tongue?" Chicago rasped, his voice strangled.

Jericho looked at him as if the answer was obvious. "To keep from talking."

He handed the jar to Chicago and moved to an old, tilting refrigerator. Chicago quickly set the bottle down and followed.

When Jericho opened the refrigerator door, a screeching black shadow leaped out at him. He fell back, reflexively swatting the creature aside.

Still yowling, the black cat sprang out of

the room. Chicago wished he could do the same. His heart was flailing at his ribs like a wild bird.

Jericho peered inside the refrigerator. Another jar. This one filled with something black that moved. . . . A mass of flies were crawling over a sheet of paper inside the jar. Jericho reached in, took the jar, and shook it. Immediately the flies buzzed off, revealing an image on the paper.

It was a photograph of a lovely young girl, perhaps twenty years old. She was smiling.

Jericho handed the photograph to Chicago. "Ever see her before?"

Chicago shook his head.

Jericho rummaged around and found another old photograph in the writing desk. He studied it under the candlelight. It was a young priest, standing in front of St. Peter's in Rome.

Jericho recognized the young priest's intense, emaciated features. It was the shooter. Except the priest he'd captured in the subway tunnel looked a thousand years older and ravaged by disease.

How the hell did he know my name? Jericho wondered.

"This guy's no hit man," he said aloud.

"Maybe he's an unhappy investor." Chicago suggested impatiently. "Let's get the hell out of here, this place is making me itch."

Wham! The door was suddenly kicked open, filling the room with frantic shouts. Jericho dropped into shooting position, Chicago at his side.

"Drop it!" someone yelled.

Jericho squinted and saw uniformed policemen at the door. He lowered his Glock. Reluctantly, Chicago did the same.

"How the hell did you two find this place?" Detective Marge Francis asked, stepping gingerly into the filthy room.

Jericho grinned smugly. "Lucky guess. What did you find out?"

Detective Francis hesitated. Finally she decided to answer.

"His name's Thomas Aquinas. He used to be a priest."

"A homicidal priest . . . that's a new one," Chicago noted.

"Yeah, well, it gets better. He studied at the Vatican. One of their alleged visionaries. Came here in '81 to St. John's Church uptown. Six months ago he disappeared. The priests up there said he was having a spiritual crisis."

Jericho shrugged. "Tell me what I don't know."

Chicago nodded and looked around. "That's one hell of a crisis."

"This doesn't make sense," Jericho said slowly. "What's a priest doing shooting at a Wall Street banker?"

"Maybe we should ask the girl."

Jericho's annoyed glare felt like a sunlamp. Too late, Chicago realized what he had said.

Detective Francis pounced on it. "What girl?" she snapped, green eyes clamped on Chicago's face.

"Did I say girl . . . ?" he said innocently. ". . . It's a guy . . . a priest." He glanced at Jericho. "Got to find the priest."

Detective Francis didn't buy it, but there was nothing she could do. Even if she pulled them in for questioning, Jericho still had friends at headquarters. As she watched them leave, she felt a grudging admiration for Jericho's detective skills.

Chicago took a deep breath when they left the decrepit building. By comparison the New York air smelled like a pine forest. He pulled out the photograph Jericho had found, and stared at the carefree young blond girl smiling up at him.

"Five million women in New York City." Chicago sighed. "How are we going to find her without a name?"

Jericho didn't answer. He was still wondering how Thomas Aquinas managed to speak to him without a tongue.

CHAPTER FOUR

The afternoon subway was sparsely popu-
lated. Christine read her book, *Infinite Jest,*
and tried to avoid eye contact with the albino
panhandler, who stood watching her fixedly.
Christine peeked over the edge of her book,
then looked away from the albino's glassy
pink eyes.

The subway entered a tunnel, car lights
dimming. When they went up again, Christine saw the albino man was still staring. His
bleached white skin and matted pale hair
seemed to radiate intensity. Finally Christine
surrendered. She fished into her purse and
handed the albino a dollar.

The albino took the money, but he didn't
leave. He continued to stare as if transfixed.
She glanced around. The other passengers
were all looking somewhere else.

"Hey, I gave you some money," Christine

said calmly. "Can you just move on?"

"He's coming for you," the albino warned. "He's coming for you, Christine."

An electric prickle crawled up her spine. "Christine? How do you know me?" she demanded. "Who are you?"

The albino smirked obscenely. "He's gonna fuck you. Fuck you. Can you see him? Can you see him?" He started to move off.

"Who are you?" she repeated. "How do you know my . . ."

Christine reached for the albino's arm. It shattered like porcelain in her hand. Just then the car lights went out.

As the subway hurtled through the tunnel, strobing lights swept the car, revealing demonic faces leering at her. The car began to violently shake and rattle. The albino man crashed to the floor and smashed into a hundred pieces . . . each piece bursting into flame . . .

Christine screamed.

Suddenly it was quiet. The lights blinked on as the train slowed and came to a stop. Everyone in the car seemed startled by her outburst. They were looking at her strangely. Christine glanced around the car.

The albino had vanished.

Embarrassed, she retrieved her book. "I'm sorry," she muttered. "I'm sorry."

But they continued to stare.

* * *

Home sweet home. Jericho had to admit his décor compared favorably to Thomas Aquinas's Neo-Inferno style.

He filled his glass with vodka and downed it. *The place is starting to look better already*, Jericho noted, refilling his glass. He moved to the bedroom and pulled off his shirt. He stood at the mirror and dropped his Kevlar vest.

Two large, yellow-green welts marked his massive chest where the bullets had struck. And they ached with each breath. Two aspirin, another vodka, and some sports cream lubricated his bruises. Like any good athlete, he knew how to play hurt.

Trying to sort out the day's events, Jericho wandered over to the window. The dark, restless sky above the city rolled with gathering thunderheads. Jericho tried to remember what Thomas Aquinas had shouted at him.

When the thousand years are ended . . . When the thousand years . . .

Abruptly Jericho turned and went to his closet. He reached back through the clutter and pulled out a cardboard box. He set the box on his bed and opened it. After rummaging through some books, envelopes, and old documents, he found what he was looking for. An old, leather-bound Bible.

As Jericho lifted the Bible, he discovered a cracked music box beneath it. Immediately he recognized it. It belonged to his daughter Amy. When he picked up the music box some photographs fluttered to the bed.

A flood of emotion rushed over his brain as he studied the pictures. His daughter Amy, and Emily his wife, making sand castles at the beach. Happier days. He picked up the music box and wound the key.

The tiny ballerina began to twirl as a tinkling melody floated through the quiet . . .

When Christine York arrived at her town house, she was exhausted.

She locked the door behind her and hurried past the library, where she knew Mabel would be waiting for her.

"Christine?" Mabel called as she passed. "Christine?"

"I'll be there in a sec . . ." Christine hurried upstairs to her room. She went to her phone and punched the speed dial. "Hello, is Dr. Abel in? It's Christine York."

As usual Dr. Abel picked up immediately.

"I had another one," Christine said breathlessly.

"How long this time?"

"I don't know . . . twenty or thirty seconds. It was pretty frightening."

"Christine, listen to me," Dr. Abel said patiently. "We've gone over this before."

Actually, Dr. Abel had been Christine's spiritual advisor ever since he had baptized her in blood in a hospital morgue.

At the time he had been known as Father Abel, head priest of Our Lady of Mercy Hospital. Now he was Dr. Abel, prominent psychiatrist with one special patient—his unholy godchild Christine York.

"You're feeling stressed," he said soothingly. "It's perfectly natural to feel that way around the holidays. Understand . . . these dreams are your creation. There's nothing real about them. You control them . . . they don't control you. Take another Xanax to relieve your anxiety. Trust me . . ." He lowered his voice. "You're fine."

Christine slowly exhaled. "You sure? Okay . . . okay, Xanax. I will, thank you."

"Another vision?"

Christine looked up and saw her mother standing in the doorway.

"Why didn't you tell me?" Mabel Rand asked in a pained voice.

"I didn't want you to worry."

Mabel gave her a rueful smile. "I'm your mother. It's my job to worry." It was true. Mabel had been Christine's guardian since the moment she'd been born. Nurse Rand— her title at the time—had served as her godmother in blood. When Christine's parents were killed in a car accident, Mabel stepped in and adopted her.

All in keeping with the Dark Destiny. *Which is soon due*, Mabel reflected. The signs were at hand.

"No big deal actually," Christine told her, trying to minimize the trauma. "Just somebody in my subway car turned to porcelain and . . . shattered." Her bravado dissolved in tears.

Mabel drew her close, comforting her.

"I'm so tired of this," Christine sobbed, voice muffled inside Mabel's embrace. "What's wrong with me? Why do I see things? Why am I so different?"

Mabel Rand knew, but couldn't reveal the exciting truth. "You don't know how special you are," she crooned. That much was true. Christine had been chosen. "You're better than everyone else . . . remember that."

"I don't want to be better—or worse," Christine said desperately. "I just want to be normal. With a normal life . . . and a boyfriend." She began to sob again. "A real boyfriend . . . just like everybody else."

"You'll have to be patient . . ." Mabel said, rocking her gently. "All good things will come your way. You'll see."

"How long do I have to wait?" Christine said vehemently. "I'm almost twenty-one. Every time I even start to get close to a guy

. . . something happens to him. Car crash . . .
skiing accident . . . drowning. I swear, sometimes I think God wants to keep me a virgin."

Not God, Mabel thought, holding her close.

The haunting, stilted melody from the music
box drifted in the background as Jericho
studied the leather-bound Bible. He found
what he was looking for in Revelations 20:7.

*When the thousand years are ended, Satan
shall be loosed out of his prison . . .*

Jericho closed the Bible and reached for his
shirt.

It was late when Jericho arrived at St.
John's Church on Central Park West. The ed-
ifice was in disrepair and when Jericho entered he saw the scaffolds beneath the
stained-glass windows. The place needed an
overhaul. The chapel looked like it hadn't
been used in years. Except for the votive candles flickering in front of the altar, there was
no sign of life.

But as Jericho neared the altar, a figure appeared out of the shadows and began dis-
tributing prayer books along the pews.

The priest was tall, with short gray hair.
He had sharp features and wore steel-
rimmed glasses. When he had finished his
preparations, he approached Jericho and
gave him a regretful smile.

"I'm sorry . . . we're closed."

"I'd like to talk to you about Thomas Aquinas."

The priest peered over his glasses at Jericho. "I'm Father Novak. Thomas was my friend and my colleague. Whatever happened this morning was not his doing."

Jericho shrugged. "Really? There was no one else on that fire escape."

Father Novak glanced at the cross above the altar. "You don't understand."

"I understand getting shot," Jericho snapped. "I don't like it."

Suddenly nervous, Father Novak stared at him. "He was shooting at you?"

"He was shooting at my client. I just got in the way."

"Who's your client?"

Father Novak's question had an urgent tone. Jericho brushed it aside. "That's privileged information. Why would a priest try to kill someone?"

"How long have you been drinking?"

He caught Jericho off guard. Father Novak smiled. "It's easy to smell. I'm fourteen years sober."

"Good for you," Jericho said coldly, trying to regain control of the interview. "Was your friend and colleague working for someone?"

"Maybe he was working for God."

Jericho snorted. "So God ordered a hit on an investment banker?"

Father Novak's sharp features became flinty. "There's an awful lot you don't know," he said, voice laced with contempt. "You think you've seen everything? There's a whole world you haven't even dreamed of. Thomas saw it. And it destroyed him."

Jericho remembered the garish horror inside Thomas's refuge. "I've seen a lot . . ." Jericho conceded. "But nothing that would make me want to cut out my tongue."

"Wait a few days."

The answer chilled Jericho's skin. "What happens in a few days?"

Father Novak looked at him intently. "Do you know anything about a girl?"

Jericho's chiseled features revealed nothing. "What girl?"

The priest continued to study Jericho's face as if weighing how much he could be trusted. "Tell me something . . . Do you believe in God?"

"Maybe once. Not anymore."

"What happened?"

"We had a difference of opinion. I thought my wife and daughter should live. He felt otherwise."

Father Novak seemed unmoved. He glanced at his watch as if anxious to leave. "Perhaps it's time you renew your faith."

This interview has definitely gotten out of hand, Jericho thought ruefully. "This girl you were talking about . . . is she in trouble? Does she need help?"

"You can't understand," Father Novak said sadly as if addressing a child. "You don't know how. Now if you'll excuse me, our hands are pretty full here."

He turned away, clearly dismissing Jericho.

"I have more questions," Jericho said lamely.

Father Novak paused and shook his head. "I know, but if you can't believe in God, what makes you think you can understand his adversaries?"

"So now I have to believe in God to solve a crime?" Jericho asked as the priest moved behind the altar rail.

"I assume you can find your way out," Father Novak said over his shoulder.

Jericho walked slowly toward the large doors, his brain churning with confusion. One thing was clear. The girl was the key. Whoever she was. And Father Novak was hiding something. On impulse Jericho turned and followed the priest into the vestibule behind the altar.

But when Jericho entered, the room was empty. There was no Father Novak—and no other exits.

He saw something move in the corner of his vision. A thick wall tapestry billowed slightly. Jericho crossed the floor and pulled the heavy fabric aside.

The tapestry concealed a narrow doorway. Inside was a circular stairway leading down to darkness. After a moment's hesitation, Jericho started down the stairs.

At the bottom of the stairway was a light. It came from a room at the end of a dark corridor. As Jericho moved toward the light, he heard voices. Then he saw them.

There were dozens of people in the stone chamber beneath the altar, all priests and academic types. They were gathered around desks and tables, reading various scrolls and translating texts. All were bent to their tasks with an urgent zeal.

Like a religious sweatshop, Jericho observed, trying to minimize the fear strumming his taut belly.

In the center of the room was a shriveled old woman, babbling in some strange tongue, her voice rising and falling. A number of priests attended to the woman. They wiped her face with wet towels, and put liquid nourishment to her lips. One of the priests moved aside, and Jericho saw the woman's arms were outstretched.

He also saw the shiny red blood streaming from open wounds on both her palms.

Father Novak examined the woman briefly, sharp features drawn with anxiety. "How many have received the stigmata?" he demanded, looking around.

"She's the third this week," a young priest offered.

"Then he's almost here."

Suddenly the old crone bolted upright, her eyes bulging—and she screamed. Her clawed, bloodied hand pointed directly at Jericho as she jabbered wildly.

Jericho froze, pinned by the amazed stares of the people in the chamber. "What is she saying?" he asked in a strangled voice.

Father Novak shielded her from view. "Get out!" he shouted. "Forget what you've seen here."

Jericho held his ground. "What drove Thomas insane?"

Father Novak hurried across the room and took him by the arm. "There are forces at work here you simply cannot comprehend," he scolded.

You got that right, Jericho thought, fear and confusion circling his brain. He shoved the priest aside and backed away.

Once outside he took a deep breath and began walking, comforted by the normal city traffic. Yellow cabs, young lovers, street vendors, panhandlers, drunks, operagoers, artists, store clerks, bartenders; all flowed around him like healing water, washing away the clammy dread clinging to his skin.

I must find the girl, Jericho kept repeating like some perverse mantra. But all he had was a picture. He recalled Father Novak's hushed words. *"Then he's almost here."*

·The priest was right, Jericho didn't understand what he had fallen into. But one thing he knew for certain. Time was running out.

In New York City, ConEd worked around the clock.

Charlie liked the night shift: no traffic, no gawkers, just the cool, peaceful sewers. His partner Phil liked it, too. Phil was a whiz at paperwork, especially when it came to overtime. Between the two of them, they had it made.

This job seemed simple enough. A manhole had popped a few hours before, most likely a methane buildup in the corridor. But it was too hot for methane. Charlie was sweating profusely minutes after descending into the swampy darkness. His mask filtered the foul odor, but he had no protection against the stifling heat.

Exhausted, Charlie slogged over to the nearby gauge.

"Whatcha got there, Charlie?"

Phil's voice echoed down the sewer tunnel as Charlie peered at the dials.

"I dunno," Charlie muttered, watching the quivering needle. "Pressure's climbing off the gauge."

Charlie wasn't really worried. Faulty gauges were common enough. And if the methane buildup went over the top, he always had his mask.

Charlie was an optimist.

A skin-searing flash blinded him—but he never heard the blast. A fiery geyser spewed up through the sewer, incinerating him instantly. Up on the street, Phil ran, but he couldn't escape the second blast directly in front of him. Trapped, he pulled down his mask and ran headlong between the two columns of fire rising up like the gates of hell.

Hell or heaven, he didn't make it. The flames reached out for him and pulled him back.

One after another, the manholes blew, erupting like white-hot volcanoes that consumed Phil's bones and melted glass windows. The roaring pyrotechnics immediately drew a crowd, but not one of the onlookers noticed the opaque shape that slipped through them like an unholy wind.

The time was at hand.

DIC - 5 -
DOMINGO NOCHE

CHAPTER FIVE

*It was more like a ripple than a definite shape. But
its cold energy was quite palpable. Pedestrians
shivered as it passed, not knowing why. It moved
swiftly, drawn by its own yearning to be complete ...
whole ... to fulfill its monstrous destiny. ...*

The green-eyed man liked to think of himself
as a realist.

Not in the best of condition, he conceded,
checking his image in the mirror. But his
hand-tailored suit richly enhanced what na-
ture had neglected. The discreet gold Cartier
watch and ruby ring hinted at his power.
And power was the strongest aphrodisiac.

Stronger than the coke and champagne he
was slipping Henry's wife, the man mused,
dabbing his face with a paper towel. The
man surveyed himself in the men's room
mirror. He looked rich, he looked powerful,
and he looked like the cold, ruthless son of
a bitch he was.

There was a rattling at the bolted door as
if someone needed the restroom. *Let them suf-
fer*, the man thought. A restaurant of this
quality should have private facilities for its

select clientele. He'd have to speak to Pietro
about it.

Anyway, after the attempt on his life that
morning, he wasn't about to unbolt the door
until he was good and ready. The man took
a deep breath. It felt good to be alive.

He went over his agenda for the evening.
First he would talk a bit of business with
Henry over dinner. Then later, he would
make love to Henry's wife, Tina. *Essentially
fucking Henry twice,* he gloated.

The door rattled slightly.

A shapeless ripple drifted through the
door, silently twisting with a deep, yawning
hunger.

Still gazing into the mirror, the man didn't
see anything but himself.

With incredible force, the ripple snapped
the man's spine, lifting his body off the floor
and jerking his neck back so that his bulging
eyes were gaping at the chandelier.

The violent shock seemed to hold him aloft
for an agonizing second, then evaporated,
dropping his limp body to the cool black
tiles.

Pietro's restaurant had the unmistakable
aroma of good food and money.

The elegant leather banquettes were filled
with well-groomed diners sporting opulent
jewels and lots of arrogance.

The kind of crowd I love, the green-eyed man exulted as he emerged from the men's room. He stood for a moment and took a deep breath. He felt great.

Henry and Tina both smiled as he approached. Despite a recent lift, Henry looked his sixty-seven years, making his twenty-six-year-old wife seem like a high-school cheerleader.

But the man knew Tina was no cheerleader in bed. There she was an ageless priestess of the sensual arts. And he was suddenly famished for her flesh.

"So tell us—what happened this morning." Henry asked when he joined them in the booth. "Can't believe somebody tried to shoot you."

The man ignored Henry. Instead, he leaned over and put his mouth on Tina's surprised lips, kissing her as deeply as she had ever been kissed. At the same time he slid his hand down the front of her dress and cupped her breast.

Some of the diners at nearby tables began to stare.

Tina pulled her head back, breathless. She looked at him, mouth half open. He smiled and caressed her pink nipple.

"Come with me," the man said softly.

Henry's disbelieving gasp became an animal growl of rage. But as Henry started to rise, the man turned, pale green eyes blank and intense. Slowly, Henry sat down. Tina didn't try to remove the man's hand. Nor did she resist. She gazed at him in rapt silence, as if seeing him for the first time.

The man slowly drew his hand away from her breast. "Your choice." He sighed regretfully. He picked up his coat and left the booth, ignoring the curious eyes following him to the door. Pietro bowed uncertainly as he passed.

The chill night air was refreshing, the man noted when he stepped outside. He decided to walk around a bit. He hadn't felt this good in years.

When the man reached the corner, he paused to button his coat.

Behind him, Pietro's restaurant suddenly exploded in a white-hot blast of flame that charred the cars parked nearby. The intense fireball consumed everything from the customers to Pietro himself.

Poor, foolish Tina, the man mused, walking briskly toward Fifth Avenue. *She blew it.*

Sometimes Dr. Donald Abel wished he had stayed a priest. Especially when dealing with his fifteen-year-old daughter, Hope.

He had provided Hope with everything a girl in New York could want: a spacious town house, prestigious private school, clothes, generous allowance. But she always managed to make him feel as if he had failed her somehow.

"So now you hate school," he said patiently. "What's new?"

"No, it's just that I hate the fact they put finals after the holiday. It ruins the whole *meaning* of vacation."

Abel glanced at his wife, Felice, a still-beautiful woman of forty-five. Felice had been a nun at Our Lady of Mercy when Dr. Abel met her. Now they were an affluent New York couple with a high-spirited daughter.

"I wouldn't worry," Dr. Abel reassured his daughter. "You always do fine. Besides, a bad grade isn't the end of the world."

Just then the doorbell rang.

Dr. Abel and his wife exchanged a surprised glance. *Who could that be?* he wondered, moving to the front door. When he peered through the glass and saw who stood there, he hurried to unlock the door.

Feeling slightly dizzy, Dr. Abel stepped back as the green-eyed man entered. Somehow he had expected the arrival to be accompanied by the blare of trumpets, or a cosmic chorus. Instead the man strode into the room and unbuttoned his coat without ceremony.

"It's you," Dr. Abel blurted out. "I

didn't . . ." He fell silent, his initial shock overcome by a fearful awe.

The man seemed not to notice. "The girl. Where is she?" he asked curtly.

"She's safe," Dr. Abel reported.

The man caught a glimpse of himself in the hallway mirror and winced slightly in disapproval. Vanity was his strongest currency. "And what of the world?" he inquired.

"Everything is as planned. Our acts go unnoticed, unquestioned. We are everywhere."

Hope appeared in the hallway. "Daddy, who is it?" She gave the man a shy smile, clearly fascinated.

"Is that your daughter?" the man asked.

Something in his tone alerted Dr. Abel. "Yes."

The man rubbed his hands together and looked beyond Hope, into the dining room where Felice was sitting. "Is that your wife?"

There was no mistaking the question. Dr. Abel's heart began to boom as he realized it was Judgment Day. His fleeting years of success, luxury, pleasure, and power had all come due at this moment.

It was time to pay the piper his terrible price.

The naked bodies rose and fell in the shadows. The man loomed above the two women, his pale green eyes feverishly bright. He thrust into Felice and kissed her daughter, who responded eagerly.

"Oh God, oh God," Felice moaned.

"No God," the man rasped, thrusting violently. *"Me!"*

As they writhed and caressed, their bodies started to melt together, one into another. Smooth limbs, sensual bellies and breasts, ecstatic faces; all shifted and merged until the man was making love to one woman.

Christine York.

Her head was thrown back against the pillow, her face glowing with intense passion as she lifted herself to him . . . Christine's eyes fluttered open and she glimpsed her reflection in the mirror.

She looked up and saw the man's mocking leer. And she knew . . .

Christine screamed.

She bolted upright in her bed, heart pounding furiously as she continued to scream, arms flailing in primal terror as if being consumed by a predator.

"What's wrong, baby? What's wrong?"

The familiar voice dispersed her panic. Christine looked up and saw Mabel standing at the doorway, with Carson the butler peering over her shoulder.

"It was the dream."

Mabel came closer, her face lined with worry.

"He came for me tonight," Christine whispered.

Mabel sat on the edge of the bed and took her hand. "It was a dream, my angel." She pulled Christine close and rocked her gently. "Just a dream."

"It felt . . . closer," Christine said with a shiver of revulsion.

Mabel looked up at the shadowy figure by the doorway. Carson nodded slightly. They knew.

He had come.

Jericho studied the photograph he'd taken from Thomas's foul refrigerator. It wasn't enough. He needed more.

He put on his shirt and leather jacket and went outside. After stopping for breakfast, Jericho went to a small photography studio on the Lower East Side.

Dan Farris, the proprietor, was an old friend. He studied the photograph for a few moments, then shrugged. "No problem. We can blow it up, retouch here and there . . ."

"How long?"

"Two hours, if you need it right away."

"I need it sooner," Jericho said ruefully. He was only half joking. A sense of urgency crawled beneath his skin like a double line of ants.

He ate a second breakfast, took a walk, then went back to Dan's shop. The girl's photo had been enlarged, enhanced, and reconstructed by computer. The faded image was now crisp and clear. Jericho saw something on the girl's wrist. "What's that?"

Dan shrugged. "Maybe a tattoo. Or a birthmark."

Jericho stared at the red question mark on the girl's wrist. Right now, only one person could tell him who she was. And he couldn't speak.

The man strode briskly down the street, enjoying the morning.

His piercing green eyes took in everything along the way: smells, sounds, passersby, shop windows . . .

When the man reached Our Lady of Mercy Hospital, he strode into the emergency entrance and continued down a long corridor, past the emergency room. A nun shepherding a couple of fifteen-year-old schoolgirls stood near the elevator.

The man paused to admire the lovely young Catholic girls, virginal in their blue blazers and plaid skirts. One of them, a pale-skinned beauty with Celtic blue eyes, flushed when she saw him looking at her. Their eyes locked, and the girl swayed slightly, as if mesmerized.

Glowering at him indignantly, the nun put her hand on the girl's shoulder and pulled her back.

The man smiled. "Almost ripe."

Still smiling, the man continued to the stairway and went up to the third floor. The uniformed policeman on the second floor didn't stop him, but the cop on the third floor blocked his path.

"Sorry, nobody allowed on this floor," the cop snapped. His hulking, bushy-browed glare held a trace of menace.

The man looked up, green eyes weighing him like a slab of tainted meat.

"The young boys you seduce have left their scent on you."

The cop's glare twisted from menace to awe, as he recognized his master.

"Remember who it is you serve," the man said.

The cop nodded fearfully and stepped back to let him pass.

The man easily found the room he wanted. They had the shooter, Thomas Aquinas, inside an oxygen tent, with tubes snaking from his arms. He seemed catatonic, laid out in a crucifixion position with his wrists strapped to the bed.

The man neared the oxygen tent. "Open

your eyes, Thomas," he crooned. "Take a look at the face that has haunted your dreams for so long . . ."

Thomas's eyes popped open like a puppet on strings. He gaped up through the plastic cover, limbs writhing against their restraints.

The man lit a cigarette, and inhaled with relish. Smiling, he pressed the tip of his cigarette against the plastic and burned a hole in the cover. Then he pressed his mouth against the opening and exhaled, filling the oxygen tent with smoke.

"They say you can see the future," the man taunted. "Then you must know what I'm about to do to you."

Thomas squeezed his eyes shut as the man cut through the plastic and reached through. He tried to pray but the first thrashing spasm of pain was so intense, he snapped the restraints . . .

CHAPTER SIX

By mid-morning Jericho managed to convince Detective Marge Francis to let him try to communicate with Thomas Aquinas. Chicago drove them to Our Lady of Mercy Hospital, but he was skeptical.

"Well, I don't understand how he's gonna tell us anything," Chicago muttered, pulling up in front of a hydrant. "The guy's got no tongue."

"He can write," Jericho reminded, stepping out. He headed for the emergency entrance, closely followed by Detective Francis. Chicago caught up at the elevator.

When the three of them emerged on the third floor they were blocked by a uniformed cop with bushy brows and a surly frown. Detective Francis flashed her badge.

"How's he doing?"

The cop didn't budge. "Sorry, detective.

No one's allowed in there. I have orders."

Detective Francis snapped like a switch-blade, her tone sharp and expression dangerous. "Hey, genius! Who the fuck gave you those orders in the first place?"

Reluctantly the cop moved an inch. He continued to glare at Jericho and Chicago as they shouldered past. When they entered, the bed was hidden behind a privacy curtain. Jericho pulled the curtain aside.

The entire bed was sodden with blood. The sheets and pillows were soaked crimson, and there was an actual pool of blood in the center of the mattress.

But no Thomas Aquinas.

A heavy drop of liquid hit the pool with an audible *plop.*

Slowly, Jericho lifted his eyes to the ceiling. At first he couldn't believe what he saw.

It was bad. What made it worse was that it hadn't been caused by some horrific circumstance like a land mine or cluster grenade or plane crash. This was deliberate. Not sadistic, but cruel. Not crazed; methodical—with prejudice.

Thomas lay splayed open against the ceiling like a laboratory rat. His ravaged flesh was pinned—no . . . *crucified*—by scalpels and scissors that pierced his hands and feet.

His organs hung down in greasy clumps and his eyes had been gouged out.

The TV played bright counterpoint to the dark horror of his fate.

"... *Witnesses say the explosion caught them completely by surprise ...*"

"Fuck me ...," Chicago whispered. It sounded like a prayer for help.

"... *And while the death toll has risen to thirty-five, officials still don't have any idea what caused it.*"

Watching through the window of an electronics store, the man followed the newscast intently. He stepped back and felt a hard bump. He turned and saw a teenaged skateboarder lying on the asphalt.

"Hey asshole—watch where you're going."

The man gave him a paternal smile. "I like your shirt."

The skateboarder looked down. His T-shirt read, SATAN RULES. "Screw you!" he spat, getting up.

The man shook his head regretfully. He thought he had a live one. He watched the kid mount his board and roll off. When he reached the intersection, the man whispered, "Hey kid ..."

Despite the traffic noise, despite the heavy construction in the background, despite the jackhammers . . . the skateboarder heard the man's whisper. Right there, in the middle of the intersection.

The skateboarder turned, just as a bus entered his lane. He never saw the bus and probably never heard the sickly thud as his body was hurled high in the air.

The man smiled. "Nice shirt," he said under his breath.

Jericho was on the verge of homicide. The huge, obsequious cop guarding Thomas Aquinas insulted their intelligence with his lame story.

"I'm telling you," the cop insisted, as the doctors and orderlies removed the body from the ceiling. "Nobody entered the room. Maybe he did it himself."

That did it. Jericho grabbed the cop's tie and jerked his head up. "Yeah? Then how did he get that last scalpel in?"

As the orderlies lowered Thomas's mutilated body to the stretcher, Detective Francis noticed something. Under the tattered hospital gown were strange, triballike patterns of old scars. She pulled the torn gown aside. It was writing of some sort that Thomas Aquinas had carved into his own skin.

She looked at Jericho. "Just keeps getting better."

One of the orderlies, a lanky Jamaican with dreadlocks, began backing toward the door. "There's evil here, mon," he declared. "Evil."

The doctor in charge examined the gnarled scars. "This is written in Latin . . . been a while since med school, but I think I can read it."

Everyone waited as he traced the bizarre cuts in Thomas's chest and belly. "And now the thousand years . . . are expired . . . Satan shall be . . . loosed out of his prison."

The doctor paused and looked around. "The next part isn't quite clear. It might even be in English." He turned back to the ravaged body. "Christ . . . in . . . no . . . York. I think . . . Christ in New York?"

Suddenly Thomas Aquinas bolted upright. For one horrifying minute, his flayed body jerked and flailed like a marionette. As Jericho watched in disbelief, Thomas got to his feet.

Bestial growls foamed from Thomas's mouth as he grabbed Jericho's jacket. Behind them the orderlies were screaming. One of them had a hypo.

Thomas snatched the hypo with one hand and lifted it over Jericho's throat.

Detective Francis fired. The bullet made a neat blue hole in Thomas's forehead. It was still smoking as he collapsed.

*　　*　　*

Jericho was grateful, but still jumpy. He needed a drink, maybe even a cigarette. Numbly he watched them wheel Thomas's bloody sheet-covered body from the room.

"I'm never gonna sleep again—ever," Chicago muttered. He looked at Jericho. "You okay?"

Jericho snorted. "Guy carves words in his chest. Someone else nails him to the ceiling. What's not okay?" He strode purposefully toward the stairway.

Chicago hurried to catch up. "Where are we going?"

"The girl," he said flatly. "I want to talk to her. See what she knows."

Chicago slowed a step. "Uh . . . we don't know her name," he reminded. "That might come in handy."

Jericho started down the stairs. "Maybe we do. I don't think it was 'Christ in New York.' I think it's Christine York. Let's run a DMV check. She might have a driver's license."

They went directly to Striker Security headquarters, where Jericho fed the name into a computer and started punching the keyboard. Images began flashing across the screen with blurred speed.

Within minutes Christine York's driver's license filled the screen.

"Well, hello there," Chicago said admiringly. He glanced at Jericho. "Sometimes you border on competent."

Christine liked to work out with her boom box turned up. It was one of her best antidotes for her hovering sense of dread.

She had a treadmill and a Universal gym set up in her bedroom, and after forty minutes of stretching and jogging her body felt loose and warm.

Carson popped his head in the door. "Mabel called," he said over the music. "She'd like you to get dressed and join her for lunch."

Christine nodded. She turned off the boom box and grabbed a towel.

She moved to her closet and took off her workout tights. She slipped into her bathrobe and moved down the hall to the bathroom. She shut the door behind her and stepped into the glass-enclosed shower. She started to turn the faucet, then noticed that her bare feet were standing in water. She looked down and saw that it was tinted reddish pink.

For a long moment she gaped at the water. She turned and saw the water was overflowing from the Jacuzzi nearby. Something was floating in the tub.

Christine moved closer and saw it was Carson. A dark red stream of blood trailed lazily from the gash in his throat.

Shock and fear bolted through her limbs. She started sprinting for her bedroom even before the far door burst open. Christine glimpsed two or three dark figures spilling into the bathroom as she ran down the hall. When she reached her bedroom she locked the door and threw the bolt.

Frantically Christine looked for an escape route. She went to the window and looked down at the three-story drop.

Something smacked into the bedroom door. It splintered, but didn't give way.

Christine grabbed a small table and hurled it through the window. Another blow split the door. Christine ran to the closet.

The third blow smashed the door open. Three men dressed in black stumbled inside the empty bedroom. They went to the broken window and looked out. No sign of the girl.

One of them noticed the closet and motioned with his hand.

They positioned themselves around the closet. Then the nearest man yanked open the door.

Empty. The intruder sorted through the blouses and skirts—no Christine York. But as he was about to go the intruder had a thought. He grabbed the closet shelf and pulled himself up.

"Yeeeow!" Screeching like a wildcat, Christine leaped at the intruder, stabbing at his

face with a stiletto-heeled shoe. She managed to stun him, but another intruder grabbed her from behind and wrestled her to the floor.

"Get the fuck off me—help!" Christine yelled, kicking and flailing. Another man came to help. He grabbed her arms while the other intruder took her legs.

"Help! Goddammit—*help!*" Christine shouted desperately as the two men dragged her to the bed.

"Watch the door!" one intruder ordered gruffly. One of the intruders hurried from the room.

"What are you doing?" Christine yelled when she saw the silver knife in one man's hand. "Help!"

"There is no sanctuary except heaven," the man declared, raising the silver dagger above his head. "You must go now!"

To Christine's surprise the man hastily drew the sign of the cross over her forehead and mumbled a strange prayer. "I commend you to almighty God, and entrust you to your creator. May you return to Him who formed you from the dust of the earth . . ."

Numbly Christine realized it wasn't a prayer. It was a death sentence.

CHAPTER SEVEN

Chicago was a bit intimidated by the affluent row of Upper East Side town houses when they reached the address on the driver's license. *Every house comes with three lawyers*, he noted darkly.

"Doesn't this qualify as interfering with a police investigation?" Chicago inquired.

Jericho climbed the brick stairs. "We're private citizens having a private conversation with another private citizen. They haven't found a way to outlaw that . . . yet." He pushed the doorbell.

"Sounds like something you end up explaining to the judge," Chicago warned.

No one answered the doorbell.

Jericho looked around and noticed broken glass on the stoop. There were also pieces of a broken table strewn about. Alarmed, he pounded the door hard.

They heard a faint scream from somewhere above.

"*Going in!*" Jericho yelled.

Chicago didn't hesitate. They hit the door together, kicking it in. With practiced efficiency they covered each other as they sprang inside. They moved swiftly across a marble hallway, weapons cocked.

A muffled scream drew them to the stairs. A man stood on the upper landing with his back to them. Without warning he whirled and fired, spattering them with debris as they dove behind a wall.

"You wearing your vest?" Chicago asked tersely.

"No. You?"

"No."

Jericho peered around the wall. "Remember, it's your turn to get shot."

Another scream jerked him into action. "Stairs!" Jericho yelled. The moment he sprinted for the stairs, Chicago stepped into the open, gun blazing.

The man on the landing ducked for cover, and Jericho headed upstairs. A sudden cluster of bullets spattered the wall above Chicago's head. He turned and fired blindly at a second intruder coming across the hall.

At the sound of gunfire, the man pinning Christine to the bed paused.

The dagger poised above her throat wavered and he glanced at the door. Someone entered. Christine tried to wrench free, but the man put his weight on her limbs. He turned and jerked his head toward the hall.

"I need time to finish the rites," he said with a trace of urgency.

The other man nodded and left the room. Christine continued to buck wildly, but the man pinning her down was too strong—and too fierce. His dark eyes blazed with manic fervor as he lifted the dagger.

"May Christ, the true shepherd, acknowledge you as one of his flock," the man intoned. "May he forgive all of your sins and set you among those he has chosen. May you see your redeemer face to face and enjoy the vision of God forever—*amen!*"

On *amen* he swung the dagger down.

Desperate, Christine twisted, and the dagger punctured the mattress. With savage intensity she bit her attacker's knife hand, and heaved him aside. Wrenching free, she rolled to the floor.

The man jumped after her, knife slashing. Christine snatched a painting from the wall and held it as a shield. The man jabbed through the painting. Christine threw it at him and ran to the fireplace. She grabbed an iron poker and swung it hard, driving the attacker back.

A clatter of gunfire erupted just outside the door.

Jericho charged up the stairs, gun ready. But just as he hit the landing, somebody huge slammed him against the wall. The gun fell from his hand.

At the same time Chicago exchanged bullets with the intruder downstairs. His precise shot clipped the intruder's ear, and the man bolted for the back door. Chicago ran after him, leaving Jericho to handle the rest.

Unfortunately, Jericho's attacker was quite large, and knew judo. He spun Jericho against the rail and reached down for the fallen Glock. Jericho put a knee in his groin, driving him back, then grabbed the intruder's hair and slammed him into the wall, putting his face through the plaster.

The man shook off the plaster and charged Jericho. His forearm smacked Jericho's jaw, and he reeled back. With surprising swiftness for a big man, the intruder scooped up the Glock.

Jericho's hand clamped the man's wrist and they locked in a frenzied struggle for the gun. There was a *click* as the hammer cocked. Jericho roared, jerking his arm up as the gun went off.

The attacker stepped away, staring at Jericho. When he lifted the gun, blood spurted from a large, fuming hole in his chest. Slowly, the man tumbled down the stairs. As he fell, Jericho snatched his Glock.

Jericho heard a woman shouting and raced down the hall. He burst through the closed door, and saw the blond girl brandishing a poker at an attacker armed with a knife.

Immediately the attacker dove through the bathroom and headed down the hall. Jericho followed, almost slipping on the wet, bloody floor in the bathroom. The man scrambled up a rear stairway. Jericho tried a quick shot. The gun was empty. He hurried after the attacker and caught up to him on the roof.

The man whirled and swiped at Jericho with his knife, backing toward the edge of the roof. Suddenly he bolted for the edge with Jericho right behind him. Jericho reached for the man as he leaped, His fingers hooked a gold chain, which snapped as the man vaulted across the wide gap to the roof next door.

Jericho watched the attacker jump from one roof to another before finally scuttling down a fire escape to the street. He looked at the gold chain in his hand.

There was a small amulet dangling from the chain. Jericho examined it closely. The enameled crest showed a red heart on a black background. A silver sword pierced the crimson heart.

The sword had the same shape as the attacker's silver dagger.

Then Jericho remembered something. *The wet, bloody floor in the bathroom . . .*

Detective Marge Francis studied the body floating in the bloody Jacuzzi with professional detachment.

"Eighteen jets, variable speed. That's what I call dying in style," she muttered. She gave Chicago a weary scowl. "What kind of girl lives in a place like this anyway?"

"Orphan, actually," Chicago said. "Both parents killed in a car accident. The nurse was her godmother, and after their deaths, she became sole guardian."

Detective Francis beamed approvingly. "I think it's adorable the way you talk like a real cop."

As they bantered, Jericho wandered into a small library area. He was struck by the impressive collection of religious books, including a group of books on heraldry. One of them had a curled sign on the cover that he had seen before.

Jericho removed the book and put it in his pocket. Then he walked over to the bedroom and surveyed the signs of struggle. He was also interested in Christine York's private world. The stuffed animals on the bed suggested a little girl was hiding inside a woman's body. Jericho's gaze went to the dresser and he noticed a music box.

As Jericho picked it up, he caught a glimpse of something in the mirror. The bathroom door was partially open and Jericho saw Christine York. She was taking a pill.

Christine looked up and saw him watching her. Slightly embarrassed, Jericho fumbled with the music box. The lid popped open and a tiny ballerina began to twirl to the tinkling music.

Christine came out of the bathroom, holding a prescription bottle. "Calms me down," she said, extending the bottle. "Want some?"

"No thanks—I drink." Jericho tried to turn off the music box, but couldn't figure it out. He gave her a sheepish smile. "My little girl had one just like it."

Christine took it from his hands and stopped the music. "Yeah? You rummage through her stuff without asking?"

Jericho's smile faded. "When I was looking for something."

"And what are you looking for?" she challenged, green eyes meeting his.

"A connection," he said softly.

Christine's eyes wavered and she half smiled. "Most days I don't feel connected to anyone."

She was quite beautiful when she wasn't

breaking balls, Jericho noted. Extraordinary actually, with her lithe dancer's body and classic face. But there was a calm intensity about her, as if she were on some unspoken mission.

"I noticed a lot of religious books in your library," he said evenly.

"They're my mom's."

"Is she a big believer?"

Christine looked up. The challenging look had returned. Then she smiled. Perhaps she remembered that Jericho had just saved her life. *More likely it's the pills*, he thought.

"No big believer," she said softly. "It's just kind of a hobby with her."

"Do you know a priest named Thomas?"

Jericho watched her face closely, but there was no visible reaction.

"No . . ." she said, somewhat confused.

But as Jericho began to pace, trying to fit the pieces together, it suddenly dawned on Christine what he was implying.

"Is that your connection?" she asked, voice heavy with sarcasm. "Religion?"

It was Jericho's turn to challenge. His cobalt blue eyes regarded her with cool certainty. "I've seen a lot of attempted murders," he said quietly. "But no one's ever performed the last rites before."

Christine wrapped her arms across her chest as if chilled. Aware that she already had too much to think about, Jericho backed off. He idly began picking shards of broken glass from the bed.

"Don't bother," she said with a rueful smile. "Can't imagine I'll actually sleep tonight."

"Neither will I."

She seemed surprised. Their eyes met, and this time they saw each other.

"Christine?" The voice shattered the mood.

Christine moved to the door. "In here." Jericho turned and saw a sleek, expensively dressed woman, a couple of face-lifts over forty, enter the room. She pulled Christine into an embrace, then looked her over from head to toe.

Must be Mabel Rand, her guardian, Jericho speculated.

"They told me what happened," she said breathlessly. "Are you okay? Did they hurt you?"

"I'm all right, but Carson . . ." Christine began to weep.

"I know," she murmured, embracing Christine. "I know." As she rocked Christine in her arms, Mabel smiled at Jericho. "I'm just so thankful you came along when you did."

Jericho didn't believe her. There was something unnerving about her cold smile and blank, unblinking eyes.

The hungers of the flesh temporarily satisfied, the green-eyed man allowed Donald Abel to escort him to the temple. They left the cab and walked down a side street a few blocks below Times Square. They stopped in front of an abandoned movie theater. The plywood covering the glass doors was sprayed with bizarre graffiti.

Donald went to a side door and pushed it open. The green-eyed man went inside. He had hoped for better from Donald, but it fulfilled the main requirement. It was totally anonymous. At one time it had been a fine theater, built to accommodate both live vaudeville and film. Donald shut the door and led the way between the dust-caked chairs to an area behind the movie screen.

They followed a trail of symbolic graffiti to a door marked EMPLOYEES ONLY and down a short stairway into a torch-lit chamber. There was an altar at one end and the walls were painted with stark satanic talismans.

The green-eyed man sat on the altar while Donald made a furtive call on his cell phone. Dr. Abel was arranging a meeting with their woman of destiny. From her loins would rise the dark prince of the new millennium.

From Donald's apologetic smile as he approached the altar, the man guessed there was a delay. But he did not accept the news Donald stammered in his ear.

Time to reshuffle my staff, the man decided. *Dr. Abel has been coasting since the girl was born.*

Without responding to his head priest's lame report, the man stood and strode out of the chamber.

Heart racing with sudden fear, Donald watched him leave. A damp layer of sweat soaked his shirt as the man walked up the stairs. Donald's heartbeat boomed louder and something pressed down on his chest, like a giant foot squeezing his ribs. Panicked, Donald realized he was having a coronary.

An instant later his heart burst.

The man kept walking, his anger mollified, but not his sense of purpose. If anything he was more intent on consummating his unholy tryst with Christine.

"I'll handle the details personally," the man said under his breath. "The mountain will go to Christine."

CHAPTER EIGHT

Detective Francis assigned two men to guard Christine York's home. Parked behind their police car was a Cablevision van.

Jericho and Chicago were inside the van on their own private stakeout. Chicago thought it unlikely anyone would try again, but Jericho had a feeling. *And so far the Big Cat's been right*, Chicago thought, flipping through *Time* magazine. The cover story was headlined: "Signs of the Apocalypse."

Jericho checked the empty street, then pulled out the book he'd taken from Christine's home. It was a leather-bound history of medieval heraldry. The symbol embossed on its spine looked familiar.

Chicago was fascinated. "I didn't think you knew where the library was, let alone have a card."

"There's a lot about me you don't know,"

Jericho said, studying the illustrations closely.

"I had a date tonight," Chicago reminded. "Y'know, not the inflatable kind . . . a real one. Not that you'd care."

Jericho didn't look up from his book. "Hey, Bobby, remember your first blowjob?"

"Yeah," Chicago said warily.

"How did it taste?"

"Fuck you." Indignantly, Chicago went back to his magazine. Jericho noticed the headline and took it from his hand.

"Doesn't seem right, that's all," Chicago ranted. "These people have more money than God, and we're sitting here for free."

Jericho scanned the apocalypse article, then returned the magazine to Chicago and began flipping through the book. He took it page by page, and within minutes he found it.

The illustration was an exact replica of the amulet Jericho had snatched from Christine's attacker. Jericho took the amulet from his pocket and compared it to the crest pictured in the book. A perfect match.

Then he read what it represented. "Wait here," he told Chicago. "I'll be back."

Mildly curious, Chicago watched Jericho mount the steps.

From the upstairs window, Mabel was watching as well. She was trying to reach

Donald Abel, but his cell phone was dead. Despite the fact that he had saved Christine's precious life, Mabel didn't like Jericho. And she especially didn't like him calling on Christine.

On the other hand, when Christine saw Jericho at the door she felt an unexpected rush of excitement.

She opened the door a crack. "Change your mind about the pill?"

"I found something."

Christine studied his sculpted, unsmiling expression. He seemed serious. She stepped back and opened the door.

Mabel anxiously called down to her. "Christine, what are you doing?" she demanded. "Why is that man here?"

"Just a few minutes, Mabel," Christine called back in a calm, slightly bored tone, as if this happened often. She gave Jericho an apologetic smile. "She loves me to death, but she's a little overprotective."

"Parents should be," Jericho said, knowing Mabel was monitoring every word.

From the van, Chicago watched Jericho go inside, then went back to his magazine. He didn't notice the shadowy figure at the end of the street.

Mabel stood listening as Christine led Jericho to the library. She moved down the stairs to get a better view.

"Look at this," Jericho put the amulet on the library table. Christine plucked an apple from the fruit bowl and sat down. She picked up the amulet and studied the enameled red heart pierced by a silver sword.

"I took that from one of your attackers," Jericho told her. "The one with the knife."

"Did you show this to the police?"

He seemed amused by the idea. "If I did, it would just end up in a small plastic envelope, on some very big shelf."

"That's pretty cynical," Christine countered, trying to save face. She didn't like being treated like a naïve victim.

Jericho shrugged. "I've put a few envelopes on that shelf myself," he confided. "I used to be a cop." He opened the book and set it in front of her.

The illustration showed the pierced red heart worn by her attacker.

As Christine read the text, a cold, familiar dread drifted over her like a damp fog. Jericho's voice over her shoulder was oddly reassuring.

"This amulet is from an obscure Masonic order, and a former sub-herald of the Templar Knights of St. John," he explained. "Very secret, very zealous . . ."

Outside in the darkened hallway Mabel crept closer, senses sizzling with anxiety and recognition. He was close . . . *very close.*

* * *

The shadowy figure moved swiftly down the street. Chicago was too absorbed in *Time* magazine to notice. From time to time he would glance at Christine York's house, but he was satisfied the area was secure.

One of the cops in the squad car was asleep, the other was eating a hero. However lax the security, the green-eyed man knew he couldn't approach Christine York's home without being stopped.

It's a damned inconvenience, the man reflected. He stepped back into the shadows and unzipped his fly. Moments later a widening stream of foul-smelling liquid began snaking across the narrow street.

"This secret order awaits the return of the Dark Angel to earth," Jericho told Christine. He reached over her shoulder to point out a line of text.

Christine picked up a knife and cut into her apple. "Are you saying that the guys who attacked me are devil worshippers?"

Jericho smiled. "Actually this book says they're the good guys," he corrected. "They're the ones who are supposed to *stop* the devil worshippers."

Christine paused. "They're the good guys?"

He nodded.

She cut a large slice of apple and brought it to her mouth. "So what's that have to do with me?"

Jericho stiffened, gaping at her with wide-eyed revulsion.

Christine's apple was full of worms. With blurred quickness he grabbed Christine's wrist. When she saw the wriggling mass, Christine screamed and dropped the apple.

They stared in disbelieving horror as the worms twisted into writhing bodies, faces contorted with agony. As if the apple came from the garden of hell.

The man zipped his fly and watched the gushing liquid spread across the street and settle into pools beneath the police car and van.

Inside the Cablevison van, Chicago was trying to stay alert. He put the magazine aside and took a deep breath.

He almost gagged at the foul stench.

Across the street the green-eyed man casually put a cigarette to his mouth. The tip ignited spontaneously.

The man took a long, deep puff, then dropped the burning cigarette into the liquid. It erupted like gasoline, sending trails of blue flame racing across the street.

Chicago opened the van and looked down. There was a puddle of putrid liquid beneath the van, as if a family of skunks had made a pit stop.

Then the van became an inferno.

Jericho stared numbly at the apple on the floor. He hesitated, then picked it up. Christine sank to her knees.

"Oh, fuck," she groaned. "I'm sorry, I . . . I have a medical condition. Sometimes I see things that aren't there. It's a bitch on first dates."

"I saw it, too."

Christine slowly lifted her head, as if not daring to believe what she heard.

Jericho nodded, and sliced the apple open to make sure.

"I've been having visions ever since I can remember," Christine confided. "I've never shared one before."

She makes it sound like our wedding night, Jericho thought. He kept slicing the apple. Nothing. "There's an explanation," he assured her.

"I hope so, because I've been waiting all my life to hear it."

Before he could answer, a massive blast shook the house as both the squad car and cable van exploded, hurling flaming shards high in the air. The library window imploded and a rush of heat sucked the air from the room.

Jericho stumbled to the window. The police car and van were roaring heaps of flame. There was no sign of survivors. "Oh God . . ." Jericho mumbled.

He had no time to mourn. A man walked through the wall of fire. Although familiar, Jericho couldn't quite place him. But his instincts knew instantly.

"Get back," Jericho cried as the window burst into flames. He pulled Christine to the door and saw Mabel in the shadows. She blocked their path, face fixed in a frenzied grimace.

"The house is on fire," Christine said urgently. "We've got to get out of here."

Mabel shook her head. "You're not going anywhere."

"We don't have time to discuss this." Jericho grabbed her wrist and tried to pull her along.

Mabel's heavy forearm smacked his ribs. Jericho staggered back, surprised by her strength.

"Mabel?" Christine yelled as the flames covered the wall like fast-blooming flowers.

Eyes feverish, Mabel gripped her arm. "After all these years of waiting, your dreams are finally about to come true."

"My dreams?" Christine protested, struggling to free herself.

"You can't run away now. Not after a lifetime of waiting . . ."

Terrified by Mabel's psychotic ranting, Christine fought back her tears. "Stop it. Stop it!"

"Get off her!" Jericho roared, as the room began filling with smoke. His fingers clamped hard on Mabel's wrist and he twisted. Mabel snarled and clawed at his face. In that chaotic instant Mabel's fingers seemed like slashing talons.

Christine broke free, but as Jericho reeled back, Mabel picked up a large bureau and hurled it at him. Mabel reached out for Christine's hand.

"Sweetie, don't leave me now," she whimpered, pleading with Christine. "Wasn't I a mother to you? Didn't I give you everything? Don't you love me?"

Jericho grabbed Mabel's arm with both hands. As if swatting a fly, she swung her free hand and smacked the side of his skull. Ears ringing, Jericho stumbled to the floor. He couldn't believe the woman had just decked him.

It got worse. With frightening power the woman gripped Jericho's throat and squeezed. At the same time she lifted him against the hot wall, crushing his neck.

Frantically Christine jumped between them, but Mabel's forearm sent her to the floor. The brief diversion gave Jericho the chance to wrench free and he wrestled Mabel to the floor. With raging desperation Jericho grasped her flailing arms and heaved. Mabel hit a glass coffee table, and it shattered.

Jericho leaped to his feet, but Mabel remained where she lay, impaled on bloody shards of glass. She screamed and writhed, trying vainly to free herself.

"Oh God!" Christine moaned. "Oh God! Mabel, *Mabel*!"

With one hand Mabel grabbed Christine's shirt and pulled her down until they were eye-to-eye. "It's your birthright!" she hissed fervently.

Jericho broke her hold and dragged Christine to the hall. The house was filling with smoke and the intense heat made it hard to breathe. They went to the stairway. The bottom floor was a churning sea of flames.

Suddenly a man emerged from the fiery whirlpool below and began climbing the stairs.

Jericho felt Christine go limp. With a dazed, ecstatic smile, she slowly moved toward the stranger as if under a spell.

"Christine," the man called, his voice smooth and commanding.

"Christine!" Jericho yelled hoarsely. He took a long look at the man coming up the stairs and his belly turned over. It was his

client—the banker. The man Thomas Aquinas tried to kill. Christine seemed to know
him intimately. Eyes glazed and lips parted
seductively, she glided down the stairs.

Jericho yanked her back. It broke the spell.
Christine shook her head as if recovering
from a blow. "No, no," she whispered backing up the stairs.

The man kept coming, green eyes blazing
intently.

"Get me out of here," she pleaded.

Jericho took her hand and pulled her to the
rear stairs that led to the roof.

When the man reached the landing, they
were gone. Mabel stumbled to the man's
side, glass still imbedded in her bloody
dress. Despite the pain, her eyes were glazed
with adoration. And fear.

She reached out to touch him, but the man
moved away, his face twisted with contempt.
Her face blanched and a cold realization
washed over her limbs.

"Please . . ." she rasped hoarsely. "I served
you—only you!"

He shook his head sadly. "You had one
simple job. All you had to do was keep her
for me . . . and you couldn't do that."

She stood transfixed as his hand reached
out. His touch was all she imagined it would
be—and much more. Tenderly, sensually,
the man caressed her face. A sexual ripple

spread across her body as his fingers traced her ear, then moved down her neck.

Mabel was still enraptured when the man crushed her throat with one enraged squeeze, killing her instantly.

Jericho used the same escape route taken by Christine's attacker. Except he didn't leap to the next roof. He used the fire escape going down the rear of the house.

Christine was still shaky, so he half carried her down the iron stairway. When they reached the ladder, Jericho hoisted her over his shoulder, climbed down, and lowered her to the ground. He dropped beside her, scanning the alley.

In the glow of the street fire, Jericho spotted Detective Francis and a uniformed cop walking toward them. Relieved, Jericho stood up and waved.

"Marge! Over here. We need some help."

As 'they neared, he recognized the cop as the hospital guard for Thomas Aquinas. Both of them had their guns drawn. And they weren't smiling.

Jericho lifted his hands. "Hey, easy with the hardware," he said calmly.

Without warning they both fired point-blank. Bullets smacked the brick walls as Jericho dove, pulling Christine behind a Dumpster.

"Jesus, Marge!" Jericho shouted. "What the fuck are you doing?"

Marge's voice was calm and reasonable. Like a negotiator talking down a jumper. "It's okay, Jer. We just want the girl."

Jericho eyed Christine suspiciously. She shook her head, confused. "Okay . . ." Jericho whispered. "Tell me what's going on."

She shrank back against the Dumpster. "I don't know."

"I don't believe you." He regarded her for a moment, eyes like blue ice. Then he stood up. "Okay," he called. "I'm coming out."

"Don't leave me here," Christine sobbed.

"Hands on your head!" the hospital guard called.

Jericho stepped out from behind the Dumpster and clasped his hands on his head.

"What do you want with her, Marge? Why is she so important?" he shouted as the hospital guard approached.

Detective Francis raised her gun. "Just the girl . . ." she told the guard. "You can kill him."

"Jericho!" Christine screamed.

A staccato burst of gunfire roared through the narrow alley. The strobing flashes spitting from Jericho's guns lit his savage scowl as he traded shots with Marge and the guard.

Suddenly it was quiet. Christine peered over the Dumpster and saw Jericho standing with a smoking Glock in each hand. The uniformed cop was facedown on the ground, and Detective Francis lay on her side, a surprised expression on her face.

They're both dead, Jericho realized, the horror spilling through his belly like rancid oil. *I've just killed two police officers.*

CHAPTER NINE

"When I woke up this morning, I thought it was as bad as it could get," Jericho murmured, staring at the two bodies on the ground. He felt used up, finished.

Then he remembered Chicago, and the anger embraced him like an old friend. Someone was going to pay for his partner's life.

He noticed something moving near the Dumpster and turned, guns trained. It was Christine, rummaging on the ground for something.

"Come on," he barked, suddenly alert. "We've got to move!"

She ignored him, hands scratching through the trash.

"Get up," he urged, reaching for her arm. She pushed him away.

"Goddammit!" she grunted, frantically searching. Finally she found it.

It was a pill. Christine wiped away the muck and popped it into her mouth. She looked at him, eyes glazed with tears. "Mabel . . . she's dead isn't she?"

Jericho lifted her by the collar and held her sagging body against the wall.

"My best friend is dead," he said with exaggerated patience. "Everyone is trying to kill us. I just shot two cops. Why are they after you? What the fuck is going on?"

"I don't know," Christine sobbed, her voice weak. "I swear I don't know."

Jericho let her go and she slumped against the wall. "You were gonna give me to them, weren't you?" she asked accusingly.

He held out his arms and showed her two Glocks tucked in his wrist holsters. "You're still here, aren't you?"

Her eyes welled up with tears. "Why is this happening?" she moaned softly. "I know I'm responsible . . . I just don't know why. What did I do?"

Jericho put his arm around her and tried to comfort her. "The man on the stairs . . ." he said gently. "What do you know about him?"

Her body stiffened. "I don't know him."

"You do," he corrected. "I saw your face. You recognized him."

Christine pulled away and tried to gather herself. "It's something I don't talk about."

"It's okay," Jericho said softly, as if coaxing a frightened deer. "Just tell me."

"I have seen him before," Christine said, jaw clenched. She looked away. "In my dreams."

"In your dreams?"

"Dreams . . . they're nightmares . . ." She kept her face averted, and her voice shook. "I don't know . . . He takes me . . . he . . . he . . . fucks me," she blurted out, forcing the words with great effort. "I've been fucking him all my life."

Christine turned, face streaked with tears. "I thought I was crazy. Maybe I am, I don't know . . . He was never real . . . until tonight."

"He is real," Jericho assured her. "I saw him before. My firm was protecting him. I was his damned bodyguard."

"I'm afraid."

"Don't be—I won't let him harm you."

She half smiled and shook her head. "I'm afraid of *me*," she confided sadly. "I'm afraid if I see him . . . if he tries to take me . . ." Christine paused. "I'm afraid I'll want him, too."

A pair of headlights swept the alley. Jericho looked up and saw the flashing red and blue of a police car. He took Christine's hand and pulled her into the shadows.

"They're looking for us. Come on."

Christine didn't resist. "Where are we going?"

"To get some answers," he muttered, almost to himself.

It seemed as if the entire city was in crisis. Sirens wailed constantly as Jericho and Christine emerged from a cab and approached St. John's Church.

The great wooden doors were locked. Jericho pulled his Glock from its holster and hammered it against the door. Loud minutes later, the door opened a crack and Father Novak peered through steel-rimmed glasses.

Jericho pressed his Glock against Father Novak's jaw.

The priest stepped back and opened the door. "You don't need that," Father Novak said calmly. "You have no enemies here."

"I'm not so sure about that," Jericho said, ushering Christine inside. "This girl was attacked. She was about to be killed by Vatican Knights—priests like you—so don't tell me we're safe here."

"They're not like me," Father Novak said flatly. "These men are a misguided clique who think they are doing God's work. They are not."

"I want to know what's going on," Jericho said with quiet menace. "And I want to know now."

Father Novak met his stare. "Put the gun away. Did anybody see you come?"

Jericho holstered the Glock. "No."

"Then we should be safe," the priest said, leading them to the altar. "According to scriptures, he cannot see inside the house of God."

Jericho and Christine exchanged glances. "Who can't?" Jericho demanded.

Father Novak paused and peered at them over his steel-rimmed glasses. His expression was both curious and sympathetic. "Perhaps now you are ready to believe," he said gently. "Come with me."

The priest waved his hand as they went behind the altar rail. Jericho saw two young priests standing guard at the door. They moved aside as Father Novak entered the vestibule.

Looks like battle stations, Jericho noted as they passed. *Might have to shoot our way out.*

Jericho had visited the underground chamber before, but Christine wasn't prepared for the feverish religious activity taking place. It looked like a medieval war room, with monks and priests working over scrolls, illuminated manuscripts, alchemist's texts— and computers. Several scholarly monks were seated around a shriveled old crone, taping and translating the woman's singsong babble.

When the old woman spotted Father Novak she clasped her hands together in prayer. Her parched, wrinkled features glistened with grateful tears as she opened her hands and lifted them.

Jericho squinted in disbelief. The deep, bloody wounds mutilating the old woman's palms a few hours before had stopped bleeding. In fact, the wounds were completely gone.

"Her hands are healed."

Father Novak nodded, dark eyes watching him intently. "Faith is very powerful."

"Who is she?" Christine asked.

"A Polish peasant," the priest said carefully. "Two weeks ago she entered a trance and—in a language she had never known—began to prophesize the End of Days."

His last four words chimed in her brain like funeral bells. "The End of Days?" she repeated under her breath.

"The destruction of man—and the Unholy's reign on earth."

Jericho could feel Christine's terror. "Why don't you stop all the church talk and just tell us what's going on?" he demanded, stepping between them. "Who's after her?"

"Do you know the number of the beast?" Father Novak asked quietly. He picked up a sheet of paper. "From the revelation of St. John, from his dream?

"Six-six-six," Christine recited.

Father Novak scrawled the numbers 666 on the paper. "In dreams, numbers appear backwards. The number of the beast is not six-six-six," he explained somberly, turning the paper upside down. "It is nine-nine-nine!"

And I shot Kennedy, Christine thought. "What does this have to do with me?" she asked impatiently.

The priest picked up a bottle of water on the table and poured some into a bowl. "Holy water," he told her. "Give me your hand."

Hesitantly, Christine held out her hand. With great care, Father Novak pricked her finger with a pin, and squeezed a drop of her blood into the bowl. The moment her blood touched the holy water it began to churn and bubble.

"Cute trick," Jericho scoffed.

Father Novak drew himself up. "You really think I'm performing tricks for you? Do you think that's what *this* . . ." He swept his hand across the room filled with monks and scholars. ". . . Is all about?" He shook his head sadly. "You flatter yourself."

Jericho had no rational answer. He watched the priest move to a desk and pick up a book. It was filled with drawings and symbols that were obviously satanic. Father

Novak pointed to a symbol that was vaguely familiar. Jericho tried to recall where he had seen it before. Then it came to him. It was the sign that had drawn him to the book of heraldry.

A symbol shaped like a question mark. He'd also seen it someplace else . . .

"*Regressus diaboli*," Father Novak intoned, reading the Latin text beneath the symbol. "The return of Satan. Does this seem familiar to you?"

Jericho stared at the symbol, then at Christine. Her eyes were wide with terror. Father Novak took her left wrist and pushed her sleeve up, revealing the red birthmark.

It was shaped exactly like the question mark symbol in the book.

"This is no trick, this is no game," Father Novak declared. "He's in her blood. *She was chosen.*"

"Chosen for what?" Christine asked helplessly, not wanting to know the answer.

"Every thousand years, on the eve of the millennium, the Dark Angel takes a human body and walks the earth. He comes for the woman who will bear his child."

Father Novak glanced at Christine. "It must be in the unholy hour before midnight on New Year's Eve. If he consummates your flesh with his human form, he will unlock the door to hell. All that we know, all that we are—or could be—will cease to exist."

What insane bullshit, Jericho observed. "The Prince of Darkness wants to conquer earth, but he has to wait until between eleven and midnight on New Year's Eve?" he asked scornfully.

Father Novak's sharp features became steely. His voice was calm, but his jaw shook with anger. "It's *not* New Year's *per se*, but a momentary celestial alignment," he said slowly, as if instructing a child. "The Gregorian monks studied the heavens and calculated the precise moment of this event. They created our calendar by mapping this event and counting backward from that moment."

Jericho had heard too much. He took Christine's hand. "It was a mistake to come here."

"It doesn't matter whether or not you believe . . ." Father Novak warned. "He is *real*. And he will not rest until he has found this girl."

Christine pulled her hand free from Jericho. "Why did he pick me?" Her question suggested she believed the priest.

Father Novak shrugged. "You were born when the stars were right. A man's body was also chosen . . . just like yours."

"If the Devil does exist, then why doesn't your God do anything?" Jericho challenged.

"He isn't my God. He is *our* God." Father Novak replied fervently. His glazed expression reminded Jericho of Thomas Aquinas in the subway tunnel. "God does not say He will save us," the priest reminded. "He says we will save ourselvcs."

"Save myself?" Christine snorted. "What am I supposed to do, get a restraining order? Sorry, Satan, but you have to stay five hundred feet away?"

"We must have faith," the priest repeated. He opened a large, leather-bound manuscript. Inside were vivid illustrations of men through the ages, battling a great beast with a fiery sword. "According to the prophecies a protector will come—a righteous warrior— to keep the girl from harm."

Medieval comic books, Jericho scoffed. *Especially the fiery sword*. "What amazes me is that anyone buys this fairy tale," he declared flatly. "Here's the Devil, with all his incredible power . . . and someone can just take him down with a flaming sword."

Father Novak smiled. "You look with your eyes and you see a sword. I look with my heart and see faith."

"Between faith and my Glock nine, I'll take the Glock," Jericho said, looking at Christine. He could sense she was wavering.

The priest's smile faded. "I'm afraid nothing less than a pure heart can defeat pure

evil," he said regretfully. "You understand
. . . you've done your job. You brought her to
the people of faith who can protect her. We
will hide her."

"People of faith are trying to kill her," Jericho reminded him. "How can you hide
her?"

It was the priest's turn to scoff. "Just don't
tell him. He's not all-knowing. He's not
God . . ."

"I don't know what's going on here. I just
know we have real problems," Jericho said,
looking at Christine. "This isn't solving
them."

Christine looked from Jericho to Father
Novak, then back. "This all feels true to me,"
she told Jericho.

He shook his head helplessly. "You'll be
safer with me. At least I can fight this guy
with something real."

The priest smiled at Christine. "You know
what to do. You feel it."

She nodded and edged to Father Novak's
side.

Jericho regarded her sadly. *Her choice*, he
told himself. *I'm out of here.* As he turned and
walked to the stairs, Christine lifted her hand
uncertainly.

"Let him go," Father Novak murmured,
taking her arm. "The true protector is a man

of virtue, willing to sacrifice everything to keep you here."

Everyone at the Vatican knew something momentous was happening. Very few had any idea what it was.

The pope had been in virtual seclusion for a week. He knew the only people he could trust were the monks of the knighthood. They were the keepers of the flame, and his best defense against the Dark Angel's wiles.

He knew he had enemies among the cardinals and one, or more, might have defected to the lavish temptations of Satan. The pope knew that Cardinal Gubbio was an outspoken critic of his decision and had dispatched assassins. Treachery was everywhere.

For that reason the pope received his closest advisor in the sanctity and privacy of an obscure confessional, carved from a thick stone wall centuries before. No sound escaped from its heavy wood doors.

"The girl is found in New York City," his advisor reported.

Although the Holy Father remained cloaked in semidarkness, his advisor was taken aback by the pontiff's frail appearance. His Holiness had aged twenty years in the past few weeks.

The pope received the news with dread. "And the protector?"

"The protector has not come."

Huddled in the darkness of the ancient confessional, the pope slumped against the cold stone wall. There was no way he could accept Cardinal Gubbio's pitiless solution. *It is not the way of God,* he reflected. *And it's certainly not a solution. Merely an affirmation we have lost faith.*

And yet, the consequences of inaction were unthinkable.

"Then we must become her eternal protector," the pope declared wearily. "Send your most trusted knights."

But he knew full well that if they failed, Christine York's sacrificial blood would be on his soul.

CHAPTER TEN

When Jericho entered his apartment, the disorder was uncomfortably reminiscent of Thomas Aquinas's dungeon. Still, after what he'd been through, the mess was a familiar harbor in a very heavy storm.

The holiday music coming from a nearby apartment reminded him that people were leading normal, decent lives: raising kids, trying to keep it together, trying to do unto others . . .

He dropped his packages and checked his phone machine. No one ever called him except Chicago. Rage and anguish twisted through his belly. Chicago's loss was profound. He felt completely alone in the world.

Should be used to it by now, he told himself, moving to the kitchen counter. He pulled a bottle from the paper bag and poured a tall glass of Jack Daniel's. His hands shook as he quickly tossed it down. *Too long between drinks*, he thought ruefully, closing his eyes.

"It gets easier when you accept who you are . . . " a voice said.

Jericho dropped the glass, drew his Glock and spun around in one smooth motion.

The man was there, leaning on the windowsill. He regarded Jericho with a sly smile. ". . . A fallen soul."

Jericho's eyes darted from side to side as he kept his weapon rock steady on his visitor. He scanned the doors and windows, checking every quadrant.

"Door locked . . . no broken windows . . ." the man mocked. "Hmmmm, how *did* I get in?" He casually moved away from the window. "By the way, you've done wonders with the place."

Jericho advanced on him like an armed bear. "Who the fuck are you?"

"I think you know. You just don't want to believe it."

Jericho paused and studied the man's face. He looked like a dissipated executive, a lawyer perhaps. Or a banker.

"I know you," Jericho said finally. "I protected you."

The man seemed disappointed by his answer. His pale green eyes swept the litter on the kitchen counter. Jericho followed his gaze and saw it all: the empty boxes of pain-

killers, the Percocet, the Advil, the Valium
. . . empty vodka and bourbon bottles . . . all
evidence of an empty life.

"You didn't protect me," the man corrected in a bored tone. "You protected this
body." He flicked his hand at the counter.
"I'm beginning to get a pattern here. Lots of
pain, huh?"

The man idly picked up a box and read
the label. "Should not be taken with alcohol.
Remember that."

Still wary, Jericho fingered his weapon as
the man moved to a faded photograph of his
wife and daughter.

"To lose your wife and child." The man
sighed, shaking his head. "I can't even imagine what that's like."

Jericho went from wary to angry. His cobalt eyes fixed on the man's face, and he extended his weapon. "What do you want?"

The man lifted his eyebrows as if it had
always been clear. "To make you happy
again."

In the momentary silence Jericho heard a
splashing sound. It was coming from the
bathroom. He glanced aside and the ground
seemed to wobble.

His daughter was playing in her bubble bath.

"Amy?" Jericho mumbled, wanting it to be
true, knowing it couldn't.

"Don't stay in too long or you'll turn into a

prune." The familiar voice tinkled like wind chimes. It was his wife.

"Emily?"

Jericho's emotions churned like laundry in a washer as he watched his wife Emily walk out of the bedroom to the bathroom. Suddenly the apartment was fresh and clean. There was art on the walls, and presents beneath a lit Christmas tree. New furniture, glowing lamps, and flaming logs in the fireplace.

Just the way it looked ten years ago, Jericho thought, fighting to regain control. *But it can't be. The past is gone. No matter how much I want it back.*

"He'll be home soon," Emily assured her daughter. "You'll see. He promised, didn't he?"

The man edged closer to Jericho. "Tell you what," he said, his voice cool and reasonable. "I'll trade you. Your wife and daughter for you-know-who. C'mon . . ." the man urged, voice warm and paternal. "She's nobody to you. You are in the middle of something you don't understand. You think you're saving Christine from me?"

The man cocked his head as if awaiting an answer. "She *wants* to be with me," he confided. "And you *know* that. You think I would harm her? She'll be treated like a queen."

Jericho continued to stare at his wife and daughter, at the love he'd lost.

"You still want them?" the man whispered. "Here's your chance."

It was an agonizing choice, but Jericho had to let it go. Let Emily and Amy go . . . forever. *He's conning me*, Jericho told himself. *He's far from all-powerful or he wouldn't be here.*

"Yeah, you're pretty good," Jericho admitted. "You can do all this." He turned and met the man's gaze with a steely smile. "But you can't read my mind, can you, you son of a bitch?"

The man shrugged. "I can't see through walls either. I'm not a lounge act." He clasped his hands briskly. "So—we've established that I need you. Terrific. You need me, too." His voice lowered. "You once said you'd give anything to have them back."

You haven't been listening. I said it at least a thousand times, Jericho thought, staring at his daughter.

"Here they are," the man whispered. "Your family . . . back."

Jericho couldn't take his eyes off Amy. "They're not real."

"Does it matter?"

He dangled the question like the keys to paradise.

Jericho turned. "Yes."

"Maybe you need to be reminded how

painful reality is," the man said with a flicker of annoyance.

Without warning the front door crashed open.

Jericho opened fire as men rushed inside. The bullets had no effect on the intruders, but a lamp shattered behind them. Jericho hurled himself at the attackers, but his feet seemed to be mired in molasses.

The intruders rushed past him with accelerated speed. Jericho felt as if he were underwater, watching them from the inside of a bowl. He flailed helplessly as the attackers grabbed Emily and Amy and dragged them screaming into the bedroom.

Suddenly Jericho broke through. The room was filled with the cries of his wife and child. Every cry punctured his heart like a sword.

Moving swiftly now, he lunged across the room and kicked open the bedroom door. It was horrible. The ballerina music box lay broken on the floor, sticky with blood. His wife . . . his baby girl . . . mutilated . . .

Again, it broke him. Jericho felt his soul drain away like sand in an hourglass. He was empty, worthless.

"It wasn't your fault," the man said soothingly.

"I wasn't there."

"No . . . you were just doing your job."

"I wasn't fucking there!" Jericho rasped

angrily. "I should have been there!"

The man shook his head. "Look at you, so torn apart by guilt." He smiled and pointed at the ceiling. "He *invented* guilt. You were just out there doing your job. You didn't do anything wrong."

Jericho turned away from the bloody carnage in the bedroom. The man's voice followed him: calm, logical, and deeply sympathetic. "You were an honest cop. You didn't take money. You were doing what you thought was right . . . and you got fucked."

Jericho paused in front of a mirror and studied his reflection. The hollow shadows around his deep-set eyes gave his sculpted features a skull-like cast.

"Where was God?" the man demanded indignantly. "He could have stopped it. No— He fucked you. And then . . ." He lowered his voice. . . . He made you feel guilty."

Jericho closed his eyes. When he opened them again he could see the gathering fury in his knotted jaw, in the bulging veins in his temples. It kept building as the man kept talking.

"Me? I don't do guilt," the man said amiably. "I embrace everybody. I didn't cause what happened here. He did. You think about that . . . and tell me who's really your friend."

My Glock is my only friend, Jericho raged. Suddenly all his pent-up frustration, loss, hunger, confusion, and righteous fury thundered to the surface. He lashed out at his own frenzied image.

His fist smashed the mirror and came away bloody.

At the same moment the image in the broken glass shifted. Abruptly the dingy clutter of his present existence snapped back like a psychotic sitcom. He was back in his littered apartment, alone and unloved.

Jericho felt a hot slash of pain and saw the bloody bits of glass in his knuckles. As he picked at them, the man clucked sympathetically.

"I can make it so it never happened," he reminded. "All for the price of a stranger's address."

Jericho intently cleared the sharp glass from his bloody hand.

"No!"

"You see, now you are going to get me upset," the man warned, his voice barbed with menace. He stared at Jericho like a green-eyed cobra. "I don't think you want to see me upset."

Now you are pissing me off, Jericho thought, flexing his bloody fist. His cobalt eyes burned like blue lasers. "You want to fuck with me? You think you know bad? You're a fucking choirboy compared to me."

"You're in touch with your anger," the man congratulated. "I like that. I don't know about you . . . I could use a drink."

The man turned his back and strolled to the kitchen counter. He rummaged through the clutter and found the bourbon bottle. "Actually we're a lot alike," he reflected, wiping a glass.

"We're nothing alike," Jericho said slowly.

"Are you kidding?" The man poured himself a drink. "Look at this . . . look at who you are now. You've walked away from the light . . . just like me." He held out a glass. "You want one?"

Jericho's features seemed cut from stone. "You need to go now," he growled, eyes burning with fury.

The man ignored him. "Oh come on," he urged genially. "You know what's in your heart. We're on the same side."

"I'm not on your side."

The man seemed shocked. "You're not? You're on His side?" He rolled his eyes skyward. "He's the one who took your family away. He's the greatest underachiever of them all," the man confided, jabbing his finger at the ceiling. "He just has a great publicist."

The man began to pace. "Every *good* thing that happens . . . it's his will. "Every *bad* thing that happens . . . well, He works in mysterious ways," the man ranted. "It's His cosmic excuse for fucking the common man. You take that overblown press kit they call the Bible and look for the answers," he challenged, moving closer to Jericho. "And basically it tells you . . . *shit happens*."

The man put his hands to his forehead as if exhausted. "He treated you like garbage. And you turned your back on Him. I'm not the bad guy here."

Then his patience snapped. With incredible strength he grabbed Jericho's neck and forced his head around so he was looking through the window.

"See those insignificant little dots on the street?" the man hissed. "That's all you are to me. Now give me the girl."

Jericho felt a sense of release as he turned around. "Not today," he spat.

Enraged, the man smashed him against the window. Jericho felt the glass crack behind him and grabbed the man's shoulders. But the man had superhuman strength. Again he slammed Jericho against the glass, breaking it. A chill breeze whipped Jericho's face and he saw the street twenty stories below. He bounced off the cracked window and charged, but the man lifted him off the floor. With a final surge of power, the man hurled Jericho through the window, shattering it completely.

The sickening drop pulled the blood from his groin. His hands clawed wildly and one palm smacked the window frame. His fingers hooked and held, despite the broken glass gouging his palms and the sudden wrench of his weight.

As Jericho strained to pull himself up, a boot crushed his bloody hand.

The man leaned out the window. "Look down," he said calmly.

Eyes squeezed tight with pain, Jericho glanced down at the dizzying drop. He was dangling by a thread and it was about to snap.

"Now look into your heart," the man said.

Jericho's tortured muscles screamed with agony as he struggled to pull himself up.

Slowly the man reached down through the window. "Take my hand—and I'll give you everything He took away."

Jaw knotted with effort, Jericho slowly lifted his hand for help. "Here," he groaned.

The man extended his hand, but Jericho couldn't quite reach it, bloody fingers desperately raking the air. The man leaned out the window and reached further.

Roaring with pain, Jericho heaved himself up with one hand, grabbed the man's extended arm—and yanked him out the window.

The man's green eyes bulged in disbelief before he plummeted, howling crazily as he hurtled faster and faster and slammed into a parked car at a hundred miles an hour. The impact collapsed the steel roof, forming a twisted crib for the man's crumpled form.

Jericho wasn't watching. He clung to the windowsill with one torn, bloody hand and grabbed with the other. The broken glass cut like razor wire as he heaved his battered, weary body over the sill, slashing his chest, leg, and forearm, as well as his hands.

For a moment he slumped on the floor, exhausted. Then he pushed himself to his knees and looked down.

The man lay in the hollow of the demolished roof, his legs splayed. A crowd had started to gather around the car. One or two people were pointing up at Jericho's building.

"Nice of you to drop by," Jericho muttered.

He slowly got to his feet, staggered into the kitchen, and washed the blood and glass from his hands. He splashed cold water on his face, then wrapped his wounded fists with dish towels.

He avoided his reflection in the mirror, knowing it wouldn't be good.

A loud pounding broke through his numbed senses. Somebody was knocking at his door.

Reflexively, Jericho went into battle alert. He retrieved his Glock and edged to the door. Weapon ready, he checked the peephole.

Raw shock swatted his bruised brain.

It was Chicago.

CHAPTER ELEVEN

Torn between disbelief and paranoia, Jericho unlocked the door and opened it a crack. His old friend stood there, dirty, disheveled, and weaving slightly as if recovering from a hangover.

Chicago tried to push past him, but the chain was on. "Open the door, man," he said impatiently.

Jericho lifted his gun. "I thought you were dead."

"Another second and I would've been. All I remember is diving out of the car and waking up in the gutter."

Jericho's mind raced back to the illusions the man had conjured. *This could easily be another con job*, he thought, keeping the gun steady.

"What are you doing here? What do you want?"

Chicago gave him an exasperated look. "Come on, man, I've been trying to find you all night. What the fuck happened to you?"

Shit, Jericho thought, shutting the door. He unzipped the chain, reopened the door, and pulled Chicago inside, pressing the gun to his head.

"I can't trust you," he said regretfully.

"What are you gonna do? Kill me?"

He gave Jericho an idea. Shoving Chicago back, Jericho aimed his gun. "I just need to know."

For the first time Chicago seemed alarmed. "Need to know what?"

"I need to know you're you."

"Of course I'm me . . . what the hell are you talking about?"

Jericho stared at Chicago with manic intensity. "You took his body, didn't you?"

"Fuck, man," Chicago moaned, rolling his eyes. "You're ill. You need help."

Jericho pulled the trigger. The blast filled the room with smoke. When it cleared, Chicago was holding his arm. A raw, red wound streaked his skin, where Jericho's bullet had grazed it.

"You're bleeding," Jericho said with relief.

Chicago glared at him. "Of course I'm fucking bleeding. *You shot me!* You are crazy."

"I had to be sure."

"Sure of what?" Chicago demanded. "Goddammit, Jericho."

Jericho holstered his gun. "Don't be such a pussy."

"Pussy?" Chicago bellowed, still irate. "That's a fucking *flesh wound*, man!"

It occurred to Jericho that Chicago couldn't imagine what he'd just been through. He moved closer to his partner and examined his arm.

"Just a scratch," he said with professional detachment. "Does it hurt?"

Chicago pulled his arm away. "What do you think, doctor?"

Jericho didn't answer. The hairs on his neck prickled and he glanced around. The room was empty. Still, he sensed the presence.

"Yo," Chicago called. "What is wrong with you? What the hell is going on?"

Silently, Jericho went to the window and looked down.

You see everything in New York, as Bronwyn always liked to say. So she was more curious than surprised when, while walking her cat, she looked up and saw someone falling from a great height, arms and legs flailing.

The crash sounded like an explosion when he hit the car. Hesitantly, Bronwyn picked up her cat and joined the others hurrying across the street.

She was glad to see there was no blood. The car's roof was completely caved in, forming a metal hammock for the dead man. "Did he jump?" someone asked. Nobody answered. They all stared at the inert figure on the crumpled roof. "I called 911," someone else announced.

Bronwyn was about to turn away and continue walking her cat, when she saw something. The dead man's finger twitched. She looked around. No one else seemed to notice.

However they did notice when seconds later, the man's hand moved. There was an awed murmur as they watched the man open his eyes, stiffly push himself erect, and swing his legs down to the sidewalk. He leaned against the car and dusted himself off.

Bronwyn clutched her cat protectively, but she was curious. "Hell of a fall there, mister," she ventured.

"I've had worse," the man confided. He stretched his arms and she heard his neck crack.

Then, regally, as if he'd just left an exclusive club, he strode through the crowd and hailed a cab.

Fear clamped his belly like an octopus, cold and slimy, as he watched the crowd below part to let the man pass. *It's true*, Jericho told himself. *The scumbag was right—I'm afraid to believe it.*

As he turned away, he glimpsed the ballerina music box on his nightstand. Suddenly he remembered Christine.

"I shouldn't have left her alone like that," Jericho muttered, picking up his jacket. "I should be there." He paused and looked at Chicago.

"I need your help."

Chicago smiled. This was the Jericho he knew. "Tell me what to do."

"I've gotta get back there," Jericho explained as if talking to himself. "Get her as far from him as I can."

"Okay, we leave town," Chicago said patiently. "You get her. I'll get the secure car. Just tell me—where do we meet?"

Jericho hesitated, "St. John's Church in one hour."

"St. John's Church," Chicago repeated. He gave Jericho a long, skeptical look, as if trying to diagnose his illness.

Jericho shrugged ruefully. "Even I can't believe what I'm starting to believe."

Christine was beginning to wonder if she'd made the right choice by staying with Father Novak. The people around him were slightly to the right of the Crusaders. Several monks had posted themselves around Christine and stood vigilant guard, while the others prayed and consulted their texts. They radiated a fluorescent intensity in the gloomy chamber.

"How much longer, father?" she asked, wishing she could go outside.

Father Novak pressed his hands together, as if pleading for her patience. "He must sire his child between eleven and midnight tomorrow night. We must keep you hidden until then."

"I feel as if I'm suffocating down here," she said, jaw set stubbornly. "Could I go upstairs to the chapel for a while?"

Father Novak nodded. "Of course. I'll go with you myself."

In the cool quiet of the empty church, Christine managed to calm her frayed nerves. She took a deep breath and wished she could light a cigarette. Father Novak was seated in a pew a few rows behind her. Christine turned to ask permission, and saw the large wooden doors yawn open.

Cold shock washed over Christine when she saw the hooded figures march into the church. She ducked down in her pew.

"Who's there?" Father Novak called, rising to face the visitors. Six monks in black robes shuffled down the aisle. In their midst was a pale old man with fierce black eyes wearing the bright scarlet cap of a cardinal.

From photographs in the Vatican newspaper, Father Novak recognized Cardinal Gubbio, one of the pope's close advisors. As the elderly cardinal approached, Father Novak knelt.

"Your Eminence," Father Novak said uncertainly. "We weren't expecting . . ."

The prelate extended his hand. "In this hour of darkness, we need all the help we can get."

Father Novak bent to kiss the cardinal's ring.

"How is the girl?" Cardinal Gubbio said brusquely.

"The girl is fine, thanks," Christine announced, stepping out of the shadows. It was a mistake.

Cardinal Gubbio turned to her and smiled, his dark eyes glittering in the candlelight. At that moment Christine saw the amulet dangling from his neck.

Red heart pierced by a silver sword.

It was like reading her death sentence.

"No . . . ," Christine rasped, lunging toward the door, but it was too late. Two of the hooded monks grabbed her from behind.

"Father—they're the ones who tried to kill me," she cried, struggling to twist free as the cardinal approached.

"Your Eminence, what are you doing?" Father Novak demanded, stepping between

Christine and the advancing cardinal.

Cardinal Gubbio reached beneath his cloak and drew a long silver dagger, shaped like a cross. "We cannot allow the union to take place," he declared.

Father Novak stood his ground. "Your Eminence, . . . you can't . . ."

Face as white as a bone, the elderly cardinal glared at Father Novak, black eyes blazing with all the authority of his holy office. Slowly the priest shrank back.

"You mustn't do this," Father Novak protested.

"She is one life," the cardinal said wearily. "How many lives are you prepared to end if we do nothing?" He gestured and four monks pinned Christine to the floor.

"We can't do evil to prevent evil "

Cardinal Gubbio brushed past the priest, dagger ready. "There is no time. It is the only way."

The Cardinal dipped the blade in holy water, then raised it above Christine's breast. Christine heaved and struggled against the monks holding her limbs.

"You cowards!" she shouted. "You fucking cowards. You'd rather kill me than protect me?"

A monk began to drone a prayer in Latin as the cardinal lifted the blade.

"May God forgive me," the cardinal said hoarsely.

"Amen," the monks intoned.

Christine screamed as the silver blade swung down.

Her scream was cut short by a sudden blast that shattered the dagger in midair. For a long moment the church fell completely silent.

Jericho strode down the aisle, his gun trailing smoke like incense. "God may forgive you, but I'm not as reasonable."

"Jericho . . . !" Christine cried as the cardinal lunged for her throat with the broken blade.

This time the blast shattered the cardinal's hand. His arm jolted back and the silver blade spun across the marble floor.

"I can do it all day," Jericho said calmly. "Now let her go."

The monks glanced at the wounded cardinal. The old prelate refused to give in. He glared at Jericho with raging fervor. "You must let us finish. If she is slain, his hope of creating a kingdom on earth will die with her. Her death is God's will."

"No," Father Novak spat. "It is *your* will. This can only lead to our destruction." As he spoke, his small band of monks and scholars appeared, drawn by the gunshots.

The cardinal didn't waver. "She must be

removed," he insisted. "It is the only way to
defeat him."

Jericho groaned in disgust and pressed his
Glock against the cardinal's temple.

The elderly prelate glanced at the gun barrel against his head. "For a thousand years
we have sworn ourselves to this. We aren't
afraid to die."

"Good—because I'm not afraid to kill
you," Jericho said tersely. He leaned over
and pulled Christine to her feet. The hooded
monks did not resist.

Jericho put an arm around Christine's
shoulder, and started backing toward the
door.

Without warning, a shudder rippled
through Christine's belly. She stopped.

"What?" Jericho whispered anxiously,
eyes on the cardinal's guard.

"Oh no . . ." she moaned, almost to herself.
"Oh no, oh no."

"What's wrong?"

Christine pulled away. "I can feel him,"
she said hoarsely. *"He's here."*

Cardinal Gubbio looked around for the
fallen dagger.

"Please . . ." Christine clutched Jericho's
shoulder. ". . . Don't let me."

"I won't," he promised, keeping his eye on
Gubbio's monks.

The great doors blew open with a thundering boom. Slowly, the man entered. He wore a long black coat and black boots that amplified his arrogant swagger as he strode down the aisle.

With each step the marble floors and stone walls reverberated. The granite pillars trembled and a deep rumble shook the vaulted cathedral.

The titanic footsteps seemed to vibrate inside Jericho's very heartbeat. But he stood fast, shielding Christine.

"God help us . . ." The old cardinal crossed himself. "We're too late."

The man paused in the center of the church and put his hands on his hips. "I've come for my wife," he growled, green eyes sweeping the church until they found Christine.

Father Novak stepped in front of him. "This is the house of the Lord Our God," he said fervently. "You are not welcome here!"

The man shrugged. "I can bear the pain of being in church. How much pain can you bear?" All the candles suddenly flared, illuminating the man's triumphant expression as he reached out to Christine.

"Christine, come to me . . ."

His vibrant whisper echoed in the flickering silence. Cold fear snaked around Jericho's chest. He took Christine's wrist and pulled her back toward the altar. At the same time Father Novak's followers came to their side.

"Christine, don't be fooled by a world of liars," the man warned, moving toward her. His footsteps thundered and the altar shook violently, sending the crucifix to the floor. "I'm what you've been waiting for all these years," he crooned. "I'm the answer to your prayers."

Eyes glazed, she weakly tried to pull away, but Jericho held tight. One of Father Novak's monks scooped up the fallen crucifix and advanced on the man, intoning the Lord's Prayer.

The monk stopped and thrust the crucifix in the man's face. "In the name of God, I order you to leave here!"

The man rolled his eyes. "Oh, please," he muttered yanking the crucifix from the monk's hands. With a bored expression, he imbedded the crucifix into the monk's forehead. Crucifix jutting like a bloody antler, the monk fell against the man.

"Get her out of here!" Father Novak pushed Jericho toward the rear door. "Go!"

Shoving the dead monk's body aside the man came closer, pews and pillars shivering with each step. Some of Father Novak's followers ran, while others attacked, shouting prayers.

The prayers suddenly disintegrated into

agonized gurgles as blood showered the walls. Jericho dragged Christine to the rear door while the man was distracted by the brief, brutal battle.

"For the glory of God!"

The cardinal lunged from the shadows like a white-faced snake, stabbing at Christine with the broken dagger.

Jericho's hand whipped out, grabbed the cardinal's bony wrist and hurled him against the wall. The old prelate collapsed, his dark eyes bulging with hatred.

"You've killed us all ... ," he groaned. "You've killed us all,"

But Jericho was already out the door with Christine.

The only one who heard the old cardinal's despairing moan was the approaching man. He paused beside the weeping cardinal, and put both hands on the old prelate's head, as if conferring a blessing.

"A thousand years you have awaited my return," the man intoned. "Behold that you have failed—and with your last breath bear witness to the End of Days."

As if popping a paper bag, the man crushed the cardinal's skull between his hands.

CHAPTER TWELVE

Christine seemed to revive when they hit fresh air. No longer resisting, she ran down the alley behind Jericho. She saw Jericho stop at the end of the alley and motion for her to be careful. When she caught up she saw why.

A gang of men and women, all dressed in the same long black coats and black boots worn by their leader, were waiting in the shadows.

Jericho pushed her back behind a Dumpster.

"What's the use?" Christine sobbed. "It's going to happen, no matter what we do."

"It won't," Jericho said quietly.

She glared at him defiantly. "How do you know?"

"Because I won't let it happen," he said

slowly. "I lost my daughter. I'm not gonna lose you."

Squealing tires cut off her reply. Jericho peered around the corner and spotted Chicago's town car. It screeched to a stop behind the gang of black-booted followers. Jericho turned and saw Christine moving back to the church.

"He's calling me . . . ," she crooned.

Jericho snatched Christine's wrist and pulled her toward the town car. He charged wildly as the crowd of black coats converged to stop him, and he slammed into the wall of people like a 400-pound fullback.

With savage power Jericho bowled aside the first wave and tore through the rest. Steering Christine to the town car, he pushed her ahead of him, then whirled to face the raging gang.

"Run!" Jericho yelled. He pumped a few shots into the ground, scattering the black-booted acolytes.

Christine raced for the town car's open doors. Chicago waved her on. When she dove into the backseat, Chicago slammed the door behind her, then slipped into the driver's seat.

A moment later Jericho reached the town car and yanked the door handle.

Locked.

Roaring, Jericho bashed his fist against the

window as the followers snatched at him like jackals. Chicago glanced back and for a second their eyes met. In that terrible instant Jericho knew.

It was a trap.

Burning rubber, the town car screeched away. Instinctively, Jericho ran after it, hounded by the black-booted followers. In desperation, he leaped headlong onto the car's trunk, fingertips clawing metal.

Chicago braked hard, and Jericho's face smacked the rear windshield. Jericho opened his eyes and saw Christine's face on the other side of the glass. The thin pane was all that separated them. Jericho glimpsed Christine's pleading expression and her fist beating against the windshield before rough hands yanked him to the ground.

Howling with fury, Jericho rolled and kicked against the horde of attackers that fell on him. He got to his feet and swung his massive arms. He felt the sweet crack of bone on bone, but there were too many. As some attackers went down, others charged him. Frantic hands stripped the guns from his wrists. Jericho kicked out blindly, but a garbage can sent him reeling off balance.

That's all it took. A kick caught his groin, and pain jolted his spine. He jackknifed and fell. Immediately the black boots pounded his ribs. Jericho twisted, grabbed someone's coat collar, and head-butted, breaking his nose. Shiny red blood smeared like jam across the attacker's face.

Someone clubbed Jericho with a bat, and someone else connected with a boot. Dazed, Jericho struggled to rise, but the boot stomped hard on his neck. The boot continued to press against his throat, forcing him down.

Jericho glanced up and saw the man, green eyes bright with triumph as he crushed Jericho's neck. Limbs thrashing, Jericho glimpsed his fallen Glock and scratched it off the ground. He fired blindly, spraying the man with bullets.

Smiling, the man reached down and plucked the Glock from Jericho's hand. Jericho squeezed the trigger, blasting a ragged red hole in the man's hand.

A moment later the wound healed.

"You should have taken my offer," the man reminded him genially. "For once in your life you could have been happy."

Snarling, Jericho lunged. The man's boot swatted his gut—hard. The kick lifted his pain-stunned body off the ground. Jericho hit the cement and collapsed.

Jericho groaned and raised his head, blood gushing from his mouth. "Let her go," he spat, eyes glaring like welder's arcs. "Or I'll kill you."

The man clapped his hands in silent applause. "So much anger, so much darkness and hate," he congratulated. He stopped applauding and slowly extended his arms. "You're almost there. Just take the last step to me."

Brain throbbing with agony, Jericho peered up and saw Chicago standing beside the man. Chicago smiled reassuringly.

"Give in to him," Chicago urged. "He's everything you're looking for."

Cold contempt edged Jericho's voice. "Not anymore."

"God has abandoned you." The man sighed. He put an arm around Chicago's shoulder and began walking to the car. "But don't take it personally. I hear He does it all the time . . ."

The man supervised from the town car while his followers tied Jericho's hands and feet, then threw the ropes over a fire escape and hauled his bruised body into the air, head down. When Jericho was properly secured, the man signaled his followers.

Using long, heavy sticks, they beat his defenseless body like a bloody piñata. Methodically they clubbed his limbs and torso for long agonizing minutes, some resting while others started fresh.

Beyond pain or consciousness, Jericho hung inertly, barely hearing the man's voice.

162 FRANK LAURIA

"Beg to die . . . ," he taunted. "Beg to die."

Jericho didn't respond, but the man's touch awakened his screaming nerves. "Sorry . . . it's not going to be that easy. You're mine. I want you to see what's going to happen."

The man laughed softly and swaggered to the waiting car where Christine stood, her hands bound. Chicago lingered, his face furrowed with sadness. He checked Jericho's vital signs, then stared into his partner's glassy, unseeing eyes. Finally Chicago shook his head regretfully and joined the man at the town car.

Through the blurred, bloodshot veil clouding his vision, Jericho saw Christine's anguished face looking back at him as the car pulled away, lights fading into the throbbing darkness.

The news shook the Vatican like an earthquake.

The papal guard was doubled, and the pope's closest associates gathered in his frescoed chambers. They approached the frail figure in the gold wheelchair hesitantly, unwilling to burden the Holy Father with the tragic news.

Cardinal Gubbio's reckless crusade had ended in his murder, along with some of his monks. The signs of the impending apocalypse were everywhere. From remote corners of the planet came reports of rampant slaughter of nuns and priests.

The Holy Father's chief advisor wept as he gave his report. "He has the girl," the advisor said hoarsely. "We have failed."

Although worn in body, the pontiff's spirit burned intensely. He understood humanity might very well be doomed. But that was no reason to abandon His path. Even if they'd lost a thousand-year battle, the truth was eternal.

Death held no fear for him, nor did hell itself.

The fragile figure in the gold wheelchair lifted a skeletal hand, sunken eyes cold as diamonds.

"It is in our darkest hour that we must have faith," he whispered, thin voice floating through the quiet like a trumpet.

Jericho's brain flickered like a defective light bulb. Consciousness focused and faded through the constant agony. He hung upside down like a sacrificial chicken, his blood forming puddles on the pavement. Slinking felines and rodents crept closer to drink.

Footsteps.

Jericho rolled his eyes and recognized Father Novak. Then blackness smothered his pain.

*   *   *

A haunting melody danced across his dreams. He heard whispers and the melody tinkled louder—the music box. A cool, gentle rain fell on his parched lips.

Jericho's eyes fluttered open. Someone was dabbing his wounds with a damp cloth. He looked around and saw it was someplace familiar.

The underground chamber beneath the church. He turned and saw the tinkling music box was actually the rattling of a nun's rosary beads. The moment Jericho tried to rise, a bolt of agony swatted him down.

Everything in his body felt broken, bloody, or ruptured. He looked and saw the purple bruises on both arms. When he tried to breathe, his ribs screamed with agony.

"So how long have I been out?" he grunted, looking at the nun.

"Most of the day," a man's voice answered. Father Novak stepped into his blurred vision. "You're lucky to be alive."

Nobody seems too happy about it, Jericho observed, as his vision cleared. The faces around him all wore expressions of defeat, resignation, and despair, as if waiting for the ovens to fire up.

"The time . . . Is it . . . ?"

They stared, hopeless and desolate. Upstairs the church was a slaughterhouse. And something had died inside of the survivors.

With great effort Jericho looked at the wall clock. "It's not too late," he muttered.

Father Novak shook his head. "He has the girl."

"But it's not too late," Jericho repeated. Inch by agonizing inch he lifted his battered body until he managed to get on his feet.

Father Novak reached out to help him, then paused, hand in midair. Suddenly he had a glimmer of realization, of hope . . .

Their eyes met, and Jericho sensed the priest's flickering faith, like an ember in a hurricane.

"May God be with you," Father Novak said.

For the first time since Amy's death, Jericho heeded the blessing.

The war room of Striker Security was located in a converted warehouse on the East River. Joe Kellogg, the chief dispatcher, liked his job.

Kellogg liked being in the command center, controlling two dozen security teams. He liked the hardware: the wall-sized digital map of New York City, the computer banks manned by his personal staff. And he liked the action.

What Kellogg didn't like was New Year's Eve. He didn't like it when he was a cop,

didn't like it when he was a SWAT specialist,
and he hated it now.

Not only did the hysteria and revelry ham-
per security, it compromised his agents.
Even now, his high-paid hackers couldn't
wait to put on their silly paper hats and guz-
zle champagne. *Meanwhile, half our clients
could get blown away*, Kellogg brooded.

For that reason—and the fact that he had
no other family except his security staff—
Kellogg always volunteered for the New
Year's shift. Just to make sure things didn't
screw up. And they always did.

So he wasn't surprised when the entry
alarm went off and the metal doors slid
open. Kellogg knew that only team captains
and his personal staff had access to the command center. But it took him a few seconds
to recognize the battered, blood-caked,
swollen-eyed figure who staggered inside.

Jericho Cane. *Of all fucking people.*

Kellogg had just received a police APB on
Jericho. *From the looks of him he got gang-
banged by the entire NYPD*, Kellogg observed.

The computer staff gaped as Striker Security's legendary team captain dragged his
ravaged body to Kellogg's desk. They were
awestruck at the level of physical abuse Jericho could endure. Kellogg was impressed,
but not quite amazed. Jericho had always

been strong-willed. That's why he was always in trouble.

"Jesus," Kellogg greeted with mock disgust. "Whadja do? Get hit by a truck?"

"No. The truck missed." Jericho tried to grin but couldn't.

Kellogg waved the APB. "You know the cops are looking for you?"

"They'll have to wait," Jericho said calmly, limping to the main computer. "There's something I gotta do."

Well, I told him, Kellogg noted. *If the cops want him, it's their job.* He knew better than to mess with Jericho Cane. The bastard was as lethal as C4 when aroused.

The other staff members looked at him questioningly, but not one of them would dare object. Kellogg went over to see what Jericho was punching up.

Jericho typed an ID on the keyboard and a small red dot began to blink on the digital map. He was putting a trace on one of their security vehicles. The one Chicago had signed out.

"I cannot get caught doing this," Kellogg whispered. "We'll both be out on our asses."

"Pray we're around long enough to worry about it."

Pray? Kellogg reflected, watching Jericho head for the armory. *Never heard him use that word before.*

When Jericho unlocked the armory and stepped inside, he felt like a kid in a candy store. The room was filled with a cache of the latest armaments. He eyed the rows of weapons and selected a modified MP–5 with an attached grenade launcher. Then he slid two fresh Glocks into his quick-draw wrist holsters. With rapid, precise movements, he snatched magazines, ammo belts, and other gear from the fully stocked racks. He also took extra grenades; a few yellow ones and a few red ones.

Finally he strapped the modified machine gun down tight against his side. It felt like part of his body. *The part that doesn't hurt*, Jericho thought grimly, heading for the door.

When Jericho emerged from the armory he looked like a battle-scarred tank.

Even Kellogg's stony-faced cool dissolved as he watched the bruised, damaged killing machine lurch toward the exit. "Where the hell are you going?" he croaked.

Jericho didn't look back. "To save the world."

CHAPTER THIRTEEN

The Millennium 2000 celebration was in full swing around the world. But judging from the images on various storefront TV screens, the carnival was turning ugly. In Paris, Berlin, Milan, London, Tokyo, and Hong Kong the revelry had escalated into rioting.

As Jericho cruised the outskirts of Times Square, he could see the hungered frenzy in the faces hurrying past. He spotted Chicago's town car at the spot marked on the digital map. From where he sat it looked empty.

Jericho left the company car he'd borrowed, adjusted the weaponry strapped to his body, and slowly walked to the town car. In a strange way he felt cleansed, beyond pain or fear. There was only his quest.

The side street was deserted. Jericho checked inside the town car. Nothing. Jericho checked his watch: 10:45, almost an hour before midnight. He was about to go back to his car when a police cruiser rolled around the corner.

Jericho ducked back into a storefront, aware he was wanted, and fully armed. The police car stopped in front of an abandoned movie theater across the street.

The door opened and a familiar figure got out. Jericho's jaw dropped as he watched Detective Marge Francis walk toward the movie theater. He shook off his initial shock and left the storefront.

I killed her just yesterday, Jericho reflected, trailing her. *Some insurance plan.*

The abandoned theater was actually an old porn palace, judging from the torn posters behind the wooden boards. Jericho saw Marge slip inside the front door. He quickly crossed the street and entered the theater.

It was dark inside. What little light came from behind the movie screen. Jericho paused and let his eyes adjust to the darkness. He glimpsed someone moving behind the movie screen, and followed.

Behind the screen lay a dark labyrinth of narrow corridors and doors. Jericho stopped and listened hard, eyes closed. A shuffling noise drew his attention. Finally able to see in the murky gloom, Jericho hurried toward the sound and saw Marge Francis enter a door marked EMPLOYEES ONLY.

Moving past dusty theater props, Jericho opened the door and looked inside. It was a large storage closet. And except for a few racks of clothes, it was empty.

As Jericho stepped into the closet, a gnarled, wizened old man loomed from the shadows. His skin was like dry white paper, but his voice had strength.

"You wish entrance?"

"Yes." Coming closer Jericho realized the old man was blind. His eyes had been sewn shut.

The old man barred his way, arms reaching. Jericho's hands came together, fingers inches from his Glocks.

The grotesque gnome lifted his skeletal hands as if they were eyes peering at Jericho, weighing him, judging him. "There is much vengeance and hatred in your heart," the old man said with a hint of approval. "You may pass."

The old man moved aside and Jericho saw the stairs. He descended carefully and found himself in a service tunnel. Phone cables, electrical conduits, and pipes snaked down the dimly lit passage. Jericho glimpsed Marge at the far end of the passage before she disappeared.

The rattle of a passing subway muffled the loud snap as Jericho locked a clip in his MP-5, and moved deeper into the bowels of the city. Hot, steamy air stuffed the narrow corridor.

Eventually the passage opened onto a subway tunnel. The foul breeze was mild relief compared to the stale haze of the corridor. But when he took a few steps into the subway tunnel, a familiar voice cut the quiet.

"That's far enough."

Jericho stopped. He glanced back and saw Marge Francis staring down the barrel of her gun.

"Put it down," she warned.

Jericho slowly lowered the modified machine gun and dropped it onto the tracks.

"Hands on your head."

Jericho complied, keeping his wrist holsters turned away from her.

"Turn around—slowly."

As Jericho turned to face her, he blinked in mock surprise. "Didn't I kill you already? Time flies when you're dead."

She smiled triumphantly. "He gave me another chance. You can't beat him you know."

"Others have."

"He's stronger now."

Because he's got you and Chicago and lots of others like you, Jericho thought. "You were one of the good ones," he said sadly. "What happened?"

Marge shrugged. "I found out life doesn't have to be hard. It's so much easier this way

. . . I promise you. If you just give in, you'll wonder why you ever resisted."

It's simple logic, Jericho reflected. *If this evil exists—then God exists.* He locked eyes with Marge. "Because we were friends, I'll make you a deal. Tell me where the girl is—and I won't kill you."

As he spoke Jericho shifted his hands behind his head, trying to grip the guns at his wrists.

"You think I'm some dumbass broad gonna fall for the same shit twice?" Marge asked sharply. "Open your fucking hands and show me your hideaways."

Jericho paused, then slowly raised his hands. He had a gun in each one.

"Okay, toss 'em to me . . . one at a time," Marge cautioned, voice tight.

Desperately, Jericho looked for options and saw the HIGH VOLTAGE sign on the third rail. He had two chances. Very carefully, Jericho tossed the first gun to Marge.

It landed near the third rail, about a foot away. Marge never took her eyes off Jericho as she bent down to retrieve it.

"Okay, the other one," she ordered.

Jericho tossed the other one to her. It skittered along the ground . . . and came to rest against the third rail.

Marge started to reach for the weapon, then realized where it had landed. She re-

garded Jericho with grudging admiration.
"Oh, wow, what a clever trick. Throw the
gun against the third rail and electrocute the
bitch. You do think I'm stupid."

Jericho snorted. "This track's abandoned.
The third rail is dead."

"Yeah? Then you pick it up."

"What?"

Fury clenched Marge's jaw as she slowly
repeated. "If the track's not active, then *you*
pick it up."

When Jericho hesitated, Marge fingered
the trigger. She didn't like being taken for a
fool. Especially by a man she could have
loved. And now she would make the arrogant bastard pay.

"What's the matter?" Marge demanded.
"Scared? Why?" She sighted down her gun
at Jericho's leg. "Tell you what . . . I can make
you a deal. I can blow out your kneecaps,
then put a hole in your gut. Probably take
you oh . . . two, three hours to scream yourself to death. Or . . . *you can pick up the fucking
gun!*"

Marge pulled the trigger.

The blast blew sparks off the track near
Jericho's foot. "What's it gonna be?" she
asked calmly.

Jericho shrugged. "Sure."

As he crossed in front of her to pick up the
gun, Jericho stepped on the third rail. Noth-

ing happened. He reached down for the Glock.

Marge noticed a little smirk as he leaned over. "You son of a bitch!" She fired again, blowing sparks near Jericho's outstretched hand.

He froze, still bent over.

"The track *is* dead isn't it?" Marge gloated. "You were baiting me to get your gun back."

Jericho's body seemed to slump. "*Shit*," he hissed. He eyed the Glock less than a foot away.

Marge was already moving to scoop it up. She gave Jericho a smug smile as she grabbed the butt. Wrong.

She bolted straight up, her hair sizzling and eyes bulging wide as high-voltage electricity jolted her burning flesh, jerking her like a puppet. Convulsively she fired her gun, blasting six spastic rounds in her death throes before she collapsed.

Jericho kicked the gun free of the rail. His boot hovered over her wide, sightless eyes. "Rubber soles," he confided.

He stepped over Marge's still-fuming body and recovered his weapons. He holstered his Glocks, then picked up the MP–5.

Hefting his weapons, Jericho peered both ways down the rusted tracks. In the distant gloom, he glimpsed the unmistakable flicker of torchlight.

Then he heard the chanting.

*   *   *

The demonic temple was as crude as His cathedrals were grand.

The altar was constructed of artifacts stolen from various churches, and stood as a mockery of worship. Obscene graffiti and satanic symbols were scrawled on the walls and the filth of past ceremonies littered the floor. The foul air carried the stench of rotted flesh, and on the altar a slimy mass of maggots covered the corpse of a mutilated cat like a writhing white wig.

But Christine didn't notice any of it. Deep in a sexual thrall, all she knew, or wanted, was her green-eyed master. The man led her triumphantly into the fetid chamber. There was an awed gasp when he entered with his bride.

If Christine could remember, she would have recognized the albino beggar, as well as the subway passengers who witnessed her hallucinatory visions—and also participated in them. However, her entire being was consumed by her master's presence. She thought of nothing else.

"Dignus sum non Domini . . ." the man intoned, reciting the Latin prayer backward. Her unholy wedding mass had begun.

A sensual thrill slithered up Christine's thighs as her master took her hand. "The time has come to join the kingdoms," he declared.

Somewhere above, a clock chimed the eleventh hour. . . .

"*Satanus beati . . .*" the followers chanted. They repeated the phrase over and over in hypnotic counterpoint to the master's words. Christine began to sway to the droning rhythm. "*. . . Beati satanus beati . . .*"

She felt the tingling blanket of her master's embrace. Then he kissed her and a moist, steamy warmth rushed inside her belly. The heat intensified, oozing like primal lava from the core of the earth. Christine's thighs parted and she thrust her hips, grinding with abandoned lust against her demon lover.

The droning chant rose urgently in the torchlit chamber as the followers crowded closer to the altar. Still chanting, they watched their master suckle his bride's pink breast, eagerly awaiting the consummation of their profane ritual.

"*Satanus beati . . . satanus beati . . .*"

The faint rise and fall of voices drew Jericho off the tracks into a labyrinth of service tunnels. A distant light flickered in and out of sight as Jericho tried to follow the sound.

It seemed as if the damp walls were whispering to him as he slowly made his way from one blind alley to another. The smoth-

ering darkness mocked his rising anxiety as
the chanting echoes kept leading him astray.

He stepped through a passage and
glimpsed the flickering light, nearer now.
Eyes fixed on the glow, he carefully moved
closer. As he did, the droning chant rose
louder in the narrow space.

The passage curved slightly and opened
onto a large service chamber that was part
boiler room, part temple. Jericho hesitated
when he saw the crowd of people dressed in
black, robelike coats. Then he realized they
were totally engrossed in the satanic ritual
on the altar.

Hand on the MP–5 at his side, Jericho entered the chamber and peered at the illuminated figures on the surreal black altar. The
candlelight heightened the ecstatic glaze on
Christine's face as the man kissed her.

Jericho's face became an angry mask and
he edged forward, hard blue eyes fixed on
the altar. All around him the chanting voices
grew louder as if urging their master to his
unspeakable climax.

The man paused and rolled his eyes up-
ward. "You cast me out," he taunted. "Ban-
ished *me*. And now I banish *you* from this
world! How does it feel?"

The crowd of followers moaned as their
master slowly stroked Christine's naked
breasts. Jericho saw her shiver like a butterfly

on a pin, completely swept up by sexual ecstasy.

Silently, Jericho moved to the altar and lifted his MP–5.

"My greatest achievement was convincing the world I didn't exist," the man crowed, savoring the moment. As he bent Christine over the altar, his triumphant gaze swept the crowd.

"*You* once asked me to bow to them. But now they will bow to *me*."

"But not today!"

Startled, the man turned.

The instant their eyes met, Jericho fired.

Bullets blasted the man's skull, spewing brains and blood across Christine's skin. The man staggered back . . . and smiled. But the momentary disconnection snapped Christine's trance.

Screaming, she bolted from the altar. The followers grabbed her, dragging her back until Jericho fired into the ceiling. Everyone froze. Jericho reached out and pulled Christine to his side.

Christine blinked, teetering between confusion and relief.

"Jericho!"

He pressed his gun against her head.

"What are you doing?" she squealed indignantly.

His mouth brushed her ear. "Trust me."

Then he looked at the crowd. "Nobody move . . . or I kill the girl," he warned. "She had last rites twice. I doubt even you could bring her back."

"You wouldn't hurt her," the man said calmly.

Jericho shrugged. "You said it yourself. I have a dark heart."

"Then stand with me."

The man's voice was gentle, reasonable, and rang with promise.

Jericho wasn't swayed. "I'll tell you what. You let us walk out of here, and I'll stand wherever you want."

The man moved closer, but Jericho pulled Christine away.

"Step back," Jericho ordered, "or I pull this trigger."

"I didn't want to kill you, but you've left me no choice." With a regretful sigh the man motioned to someone in the crowd. A familiar figure stepped into view, his gun leveled at Jericho.

"Let her go," Chicago said wearily.

Jericho shifted his aim to Chicago, eyes blazing with anger and betrayal.

Chicago knew what he was thinking. "You'd be amazed at what you agree to when you're on fire."

"Don't do this, Bobby. You're better than this—better than him!"

Chicago's weapon didn't waver.

"Besides," Jericho challenged. "You'll never get the first shot off."

Chicago knew it was true. Jericho was lightning fast. He also knew his partner had found something even stronger.

Faith. Chicago missed it profoundly. He looked over his shoulder and saw the man glaring. Cowed, Chicago squinted down the barrel of his gun. His eyes met Jericho's and suddenly he realized something. *Why doesn't he kill Jericho himself?*

Fighting back the fear, Chicago lowered his gun.

"Bobbeee . . . ," the man called. "We had a deal."

Defiantly, Chicago shook his head.

At that precise moment, a breeze of fresh power blew through Jericho's pain-stiffened limbs.

"Very well, the deal's off," the man snapped, visibly annoyed. He reached out and brushed Chicago's arm with a finger, as if striking a match.

Chicago shrieked in agony as his arm burst into flame. Within seconds his entire body was on fire, skin bubbling and sizzling as he spun madly, yowling for death. The hot stench of his burning flesh sent a surge of nausea into Jericho's throat.

"No!" Jericho bellowed in helpless rage.

He jammed a red grenade into the launcher and fired.

The grenade imbedded itself in the man's chest. For a nanosecond the man gaped at the finned object protruding from his heart like a small red shark.

Then it exploded. The hot, jolting blast ripped his head, shoulder, and one arm from the rest of his torso. In the roaring chaos, Jericho grabbed Christine's wrist and pulled her through the smoke and confusion.

The followers scattered as Jericho hustled Christine to the door. Reflexively, Jericho turned to cover their retreat. He locked another grenade, his launcher aimed directly at the burning altar . . . and icy shock clubbed his brain.

Frozen with awed terror, Jericho watched the man's head and arm scuttle across the floor like a one-clawed crab—and reattach to the mutilated torso at the base of the altar. As the ragged chunks of flesh merged and healed, the man cocked his head at Jericho.

"You're just delaying the inevitable," he mocked, getting to his feet.

CHAPTER FOURTEEN

Jericho glanced up at the thick red gas pipe traveling through the metallic web above the chamber. And fired.

The grenade blast shattered the pipe, unleashing a huge fiery cloud that incinerated the chamber and flooded into the tunnel.

"Move!" Jericho shouted as the firestorm rushed closer, swirling flames licking at their heels. The howling fireball sucked the air from the cramped space as they raced desperately down the tunnel, their scorched lungs heaving.

Jericho pulled Christine around a corner to escape the rolling flames, but the searing heat stressed the metal pipes to their breaking point. Rivets popped, strafing the walls like bullets, as superheated fumes boiled into the already steaming tunnel.

Staggering under the oppressive weight of

airless heat, Jericho dragged Christine through the catacombs.

A moment later, the green-eyed man emerged from the raging holocaust behind them.

Both Jericho and Christine felt him coming.

The man's presence pulsed in their skulls like an abscessed tooth, draining their energy as they scrambled to escape. Jericho skidded to a stop when he saw the figures in long coats emerge from the shadows ahead. They were trapped.

Jericho leveled his Glock at the people blocking the tunnel and fired, opening a path. But the man was still behind them.

"What do we do now?" Christine asked breathlessly.

Jericho shrugged. "I'm thinking."

Without warning Christine grabbed his hand and pulled the Glock to her head. "I won't be responsible for the end of the world."

As Christine's finger squeezed the trigger he yanked the gun aside. "I may not be the most religious man, but I know that killing yourself is a sin," Jericho said hoarsely. "Dying like that—he could bring you back. You'd be delivering yourself to him."

"Then for Chrissakes—*you do it!*" she

sobbed. "What's there for me to live for anyway?"

Jericho smiled. "It's New Year's Eve."

She turned and started running. *No sense of humor*, Jericho lamented chasing after her. She darted into a corridor. Jericho followed, aware of the rumbling approach of a subway train. Behind them, the man stalked closer.

Christine stumbled through an opening and found herself in a subway tunnel. Her churning senses were focused on one desperate need: to escape the man's compelling power.

But when she emerged onto the tracks, a screeching spotlight pinned her like a deer. Transfixed, she watched the screaming subway train descend on her.

Suddenly, Jericho's weight forced her down between the tracks. A deafening boom roared over them like a tornado in a junkyard. Christine tried to lift her head but Jericho pushed her face into the wet cinders as the subway cars thundered over them.

The train roared over them like a sudden squall. Jericho felt a rush of cool air and looked up. The subway had passed and was skidding to a stop. Lifting his head he saw the train had only two cars. His eyes met Christine's. She was crying, not in fear, but in anger.

"You should have ended it," Christine

sobbed. "You should have just let it end."

Jericho grabbed her shoulders and put his face close to hers. "Look at me!" he rasped, each breath painful. "Look at me! Whatever it takes . . . we're gonna get . . . through this."

"How do you know that?"

Jericho slowly stood up and pulled Christine to her feet.

"Show a little faith," he growled.

A slash of light fell across the tracks. Jericho looked up and saw the rear door of the subway open. At the same time a shuffling sound came from the darkness behind them. Immediately Jericho began running to the subway train, dragging Christine along.

The motorman's expression tilted from relief to amazement as Jericho and Christine hobbled out of the shadows and mounted the rear platform.

"I thought I hit you," the motorman said gratefully. Then he got a good look at Jericho. The sweaty, muscular figure climbing aboard bristled with lethal weaponry. His bruised, wounded body moved like an aroused predator, nostrils flaring and eyes crazed.

"Get us out of here—*now!*"

The motorman cringed as Jericho lifted his machine gun and began firing. Then the motorman glimpsed the figures in black running in and out of the light . . . coming closer.

Jericho pushed Christine through the door, grabbed the terrified motorman, and raced to the front of the train. He pushed the motorman into his compartment and took a position at the front window. He checked his weapons, inserted fresh clips, and locked a grenade in the launcher.

Finally Jericho stepped into the motorman's compartment. "Why aren't we moving?"

The motorman's puffy white face gleamed with sweat. "After an emergency stop I have to restart the system."

"How long?"

"Just give me a minute," the motorman pleaded, fumbling with the switches on the console.

"Jer!"

Jericho pivoted, alerted by the fear in Christine's voice. A handful of followers had boarded the train and were making their way into the front car. With a quick burst he cut down the first three intruders, and the rest retreated. As if sweeping rats in a barn, Jericho fired another burst down the corridor, driving the survivors off the train.

He ran to the rear car, closely trailed by Christine. He fired a few more rounds into the tunnel, keeping the black-coated zealots back.

Christine folded her arms as if chilled. "I'd

feel better if you could show me how to use one of those things."

So you can blow your brains out? No thanks, Jericho brooded, eyes scanning the tunnel.

"I just want to help," she said calmly. "I want to do something."

Something in her voice swayed him. He glanced down and searched her tear-streaked face. "And you won't . . . ?"

Christine gave him a wry smile. "Have a little faith."

Jericho heard that. Carefully he handed her one of his Glocks. She took it gingerly as if expecting it to go off.

It's her first time. Good sign, Jericho noted. He stood behind her and helped her grip the gun properly. "Just line them up in the cross-hairs and squeeze," he said crisply. "But be ready for the recoil."

She squeezed. *Click . . . click . . . click . . . click.*

"Just like that," he congratulated. He took a fresh clip and showed her how to snap it in and cock the hammer. "Here's the safety," he added. "Leave it on until you . . ."

Christine pointed the gun at his head— and fired.

Jericho ducked, jerking his MP–5 at Christine. *"What* are you . . . ?" Then he saw the angle of her weapon and looked up. An attacker hung upside down from the roof like a long black flag.

"Like that?" Christine asked innocently.

Jericho scanned the tunnel. "Yes—like that." As if punctuating his praise, Jericho fired three quick shots.

Christine moved to his shoulder and saw the black-coated figures. They darted in and out of the darkness, like a writhing black snake with white spots. She aimed at the nearest white spot and squeezed. The recoil staggered her. She planted her feet, gripped tight with both hands, and fired. This time she absorbed the kick. She also hit her target. One of the attackers fell across the tracks.

Jericho nodded approvingly, and put a few more shots into the shadows. The white spots shrank back, then reappeared, coiling between the nearby pillars.

Jericho fired and heard the twang of bullets bouncing off steel.

A white face came out of the shadows, charging for the platform. The attacker stopped short, brains and blood spewing from his skull like dirty toothpaste. *Nice shot*, Jericho noted with professional pride as he ran to the front car.

"Get us moving!" Jericho ordered. He blasted a hole in the roof to make his point.

"Got it!" the motorman cried hoarsely. He

threw the lever and the train lurched forward.

The *crack* of Christine's gun drew Jericho back to the rear platform. He sprayed the tracks with bullets as the train slowly gathered speed. Ignoring the gunfire, a horde of black-coated zealots spilled out of the shadows and ran after the departing train, their pale faces twisted with demonic frenzy.

"This city has really gone to hell," Jericho said grimly, watching them fade as the train picked up speed.

With only two cars to pull, the light train flew down the tunnel, its headlights drilling through the darkness. Jericho and Christine stood at the front window, staring at the rushing tracks as the subway rattled toward salvation.

They both saw it at the same time. The train rounded a corner and the lights revealed a figure standing on the tracks, arms crossed.

"Oh God!" Christine moaned. "He's here!"

Jericho was already inside the motorman's compartment. He pulled the motorman's hand away from the brake lever, and pushed the throttle up. The train swayed as it accelerated, careening directly at the man standing dead ahead.

Arms crossed with casual arrogance, the man remained where he was.

The train kept accelerating and Jericho kept his hand on the throttle. When they were a few feet away, Jericho saw the man smile.

"Hang on!" Jericho yelled. An instant later the train slammed into the man like a moth on a windshield. Jericho felt a slight jump as the heavy steel wheels ran over the body.

CHAPTER FIFTEEN

Jericho raced down the length of the first car and through the second car. Wind whistling around him, he stood on the rear platform and peered along the tracks.

They were empty.

Christine came up behind him. Jericho shrugged helplessly.

"He's gone."

They looked at each other, knowing the truth, but unwilling to admit it.

The floor burst open and an arm crashed through, clawing at Christine's ankle. Jericho's MP–5 shattered Christine's scream as his bullets chewed the floor.

The arm retreated. A moment later it was back, smashing down through the roof and snatching at Christine's hair.

Jericho and Christine began firing at the roof as they backed into the lead car. They hurried up front to the motorman.

"We have to disconnect the car!" Jericho declared breathlessly.

The motorman blinked. "What are you talking about?"

Jericho waved his gun toward the rear car. "He's back there!"

"Who?" the motorman quavered, totally unstrung.

Before Jericho could answer, the motorman arched sharply, like a bow being bent. Glass and metal splintered as a fist speared the front of the train, impaling the motorman's heart. A fountain of blood spattered the control panel.

The motorman screeched in agony as the fist yanked him through the broken window. Unable to save him, Jericho and Christine fired madly, adrenaline pumping with terror.

Jericho pushed Christine back as the train continued to hurtle through the darkness. As they passed between cars, Jericho glanced down and saw the coupling mechanism that hitched them together.

Shoving Christine through the door, Jericho balanced between the rocking subways cars, and spotted a lever near the coupling hitch. Jericho reached down and pulled the lever with both arms, biceps straining against the rigid steel.

Jericho heaved and the lever gave. An

abrupt shower of sparks lit up the darkness as metal ground on metal and the cars separated.

Suddenly Jericho realized he was on the wrong car.

Christine's car slowed and his own car surged ahead. In less than a second the gap yawned from two to six feet.

Without thinking, Jericho tried a running jump across the widening gap. The rear car slowed and Jericho didn't quite make it.

His hands clutched the side rails, and his feet kicked vainly in midair. Christine swooped down and grabbed his shirt. With her help, he pulled himself onto the rear car and looked back.

The lead car was rapidly moving further away, as their car drifted to a stop. But they could see the man, his long black coattails trailing in the wind as he trotted to the rear of his car, his glaring green eyes fixed on Jericho.

"Jericho!" he called, voice booming. "I shall cast you into hell like my father did to me at the dawn of time."

"Times change!" Jericho yelled defiantly, locking a red warhead in his launcher. "Welcome to the twenty-first century!"

Enraged the man broke into a run. When his foot hit the rear platform, he leaped, hands clawing the roaring air.

In that instant Jericho fired, blasting the man back into his subway car, a hot grenade buried in his belly. Then it exploded.

Flaring like a fiery balloon, the subway car blew to smithereens. Jericho pulled Christine to the floor, covering her against the rolling fireball that rushed over them like hell's hot breath.

Long moments later they drifted to a stop. Jericho pushed himself up and peered down the track. Fifty yards ahead yellow flames consumed the wrecked car like a funeral pyre.

Blood surging through his body, Jericho pumped another grenade into the flaming wreckage, and another—bright white thunderbolts pounding the tunnel walls.

Then it was quiet except for the faint sizzle of twisted rubble burning in the darkness ahead. Christine slowly got to her feet, face glowing with relief.

Jericho helped her off the car and they hurried back along the tracks. But as they fled, a familiar voice bellowed after them.

"For thirty thousand years I've walked through the hearts and minds of men," the voice blared, echoing from every wall and crevice around them. "I have built the gas ovens at Auschwitz, I have haunted the killing fields of Cambodia, and I've spurred good Christians in Serbia to rape and loot in the name of their Lord."

The man's arrogant laughter mocked Jericho's frantic scrambling to find a way out. "I lit the fire that made Troy burn," he boasted. "I stood by and watched mankind nail the son of God to a wooden cross, and I was there in the beginning . . . on the Tree of Life. So how can you expect to defeat me when *I am forever*—and you are just a man?"

The question rattled through Jericho's exhausted awareness as he glimpsed the faint red lights of an emergency exit. Dragging Christine along, he crossed the tracks and pushed through the metal door.

Cool fresh air washed over them as they emerged from the subway access onto the street. A few blocks away they could see the police lights and barricades of the New Year celebration.

But as Jericho and Christine headed for the lights, menacing figures clad in long black coats came out of darkened storefronts. Jericho started across the street, then saw a manhole cover lifting. With mounting alarm Jericho watched more of the shadowy figures spill onto the street from manholes, sewer gratings, doorways—until all escape routes were cut off.

As the black-clad followers closed in, Jericho frantically looked for sanctuary. He saw a church nearby and bolted for it, pulling Christine with him. They raced up the stone stairs and went inside, slamming the doors behind them.

The church was deserted. The only light came from a crystal chandelier high above the massive, ornately carved altar. A few tall candles flickered on either side of the altar. Jericho found a cast-iron candle holder and wedged it between the door latches. "The other doors," he grunted. "Block them."

Christine ran to the door on one side of the altar. She pulled a candle from its holder and jammed the metal rod in the latches. Jericho did the same on the other side. They reunited in front of the altar.

Dazed with fear and exhaustion, Christine shrank against Jericho's heaving chest as the church doors began to crash and shudder. Shoulders jarred against the doors, fists banged; the clamor became louder, rising to a hammering cacophony that shattered Christine's nerves.

Abruptly, thick silence blanketed the gloomy chapel. A sensual calm stole over Christine's terror, oozing through her belly like warm honey.

"I can feel him . . . ," she whispered. "He's coming."

Jericho hefted his grenade launcher. "Hide."

"But . . ."

"Hide!" Jericho snapped. He pushed Christine to the rear of the chapel. She hurried to find cover, crouching behind a silver crucifix on the high altar.

Jericho took a warhead from his ammo belt. Jaw clenched, he slid the grenade on the launcher. As he glanced around for cover he noticed a life-sized statue of Michael the Archangel nearby. Michael's Sword of Faith thrust up to God, his foot planted victoriously on the slain Beast.

And this is my Sword of Faith, Jericho reflected grimly, locking the warhead.

But his fingers performed the practiced task slowly, almost . . . reluctantly. Jericho looked around the chapel, noticing for the first time its magnificent stained-glass windows. The windows seemed illuminated by some strange light, enhancing the brilliantly colored images of the holy saints. Their benign faces seemed alive, beaming down their blessings on Jericho on the cusp of his great battle.

Jericho's eyes traveled down to the altar and the statue of the Madonna, her radiant smile beaming encouragement in his moment of truth.

And the truth is I'm totally alone, Jericho

thought, finger scratching at the trigger. He looked up and saw the lone figure on the cross above the altar; crucified for the sins of man.

A distant rumble shook the marble floor. At that moment Jericho realized that all his weapons were useless against the approaching horror. Twice he had slammed a grenade directly into the man's body. Twice the blast incinerated the man's shredded flesh. And yet he was back.

It'll take something much more powerful, Jericho reflected wearily. *A strength I don't have.*

The rumbling grew louder.

He bowed his head and tossed his weapon aside. As the MP–5 clattered against the marble floor, he lifted his eyes to heaven.

"Please, dear God," Jericho said softly. "Help me."

A profound silence fell over the chapel like snow. Jericho teetered at the edge of his life and felt a gust of fresh wind blow across his fevered skin. He took a long, healing breath.

The floor suddenly jolted as if swatted by a giant fist. The rumbling intensified, shaking stones from buttresses overhead. The falling stones crashed against the heaving marble floor. Statues broke free of their masonry and fell around him like slain soldiers.

Without warning the stained-glass windows imploded.

The thundering blast showered the church with broken glass. Instinctively Jericho covered his head and ducked. As he turned, he saw the rear pews swell up and ripple towards him. Row after row of pews rose up, roaring closer like an invisible wave.

Jericho lowered his arms and stood where he was.

The floor buckled and cracked. Pew benches flew up one after another, rushing straight at Jericho.

Suddenly it went dark as the chandelier wrenched loose in a swirl of sparks and exploded against the ground. But the impact was swallowed by a sky-shattering boom when the evil presence emerged.

Jericho staggered back, belly frozen with awe as a noxious black ooze erupted from the floor like an oily cloud .twisting into forms that dissolved into the darkness. The stench of rotted flesh fouled the chapel and Jericho saw an eye gleaming through the ooze.

The flat, venomous gaze of a reptile gleamed at him through the fetid blackness. The reptilian eye loomed over Jericho, weaving hypnotically as it grew larger, its slithering presence uncoiling. Like the shuddering hiss of a hurricane wind, its steamy breath flooded over him, warm and slimy.

Jericho's awe melted to animal terror. He crouched back, hands reaching for his discarded weapon. Then he stopped and slowly stood up.

It wants me to be afraid, Jericho realized, fear draining away. *It wants me to kill. It feeds on it, feeds on everyone's fear. That's its true power.*

Jericho spread his arms wide in a welcoming embrace.

"You need a body," Jericho said calmly. "Take mine."

With stunning force it pounced. Jericho's head snapped back as he was hurled against a pillar. Brutally it took possession of his flesh, scratching beneath his skin, burrowing into his veins, poisoning his bloodstream. Jericho's eyes rolled up in convulsive agony as it squeezed into his skull, the pressure twisting every nerve in his brain until the pain tumbled into an endless void.

And he ceased to exist.

CHAPTER SIXTEEN

Christine saw it all from her hiding place behind the altar.

Already terrified, she numbly watched Jericho prepare himself for battle. She saw him lift his head, deep-set eyes scanning the chapel, his expression radiant with some strange energy. Then he did something that speared her with raw horror.

Jericho threw his weapon to the ground.

A peaceful silence settled over the chapel.

At that instant all hell erupted. The stained-glass windows exploded, pew benches flew up like toothpicks, the chandelier crashed to the floor, and boiling darkness closed in.

Christine covered her head as stone and glass pelted the trembling altar. A foul odor fumed through the chaos, flooding her throat with nausea.

Suddenly it was quiet.

Dazed, Christine slowly emerged from behind the altar. Her nausea dissolved and she felt a faint sense of exhilaration. As her eyes adjusted to the dim, dusty light, she saw Jericho's lifeless body splayed against a pillar.

Christine glanced around the ominous darkness, then hurried to Jericho's side. She knelt beside him, fingers hovering uncertainly above his bruised face.

"Jericho!" she moaned urgently. *"Jer!"*

His eyes blinked open.

"You okay?" Christine asked, breathless with relief. "What happened?"

A slow, sweet smile spread across his stony features. "It's over," he told her. *"We won."*

Christine pulled him into her arms, holding him tight. "Thank God," she said with hushed fervor. "Thank God."

Jericho pulled away and got to his feet . "Let's go," he said softly, extending his hand. She stood up and started toward the door.

Firmly—too firmly—Jericho stopped her.

"What's wrong?" she whispered.

Without answering, he started dragging her to the altar.

"Jericho!" she screamed, feet digging into the ground.

"Nothing's wrong," he assured, pulling

her closer to the altar. "Everything's how it should be . . ."

Christine heard something chilling in his droning voice. It wasn't Jericho. Still struggling, she peered into his face. It had changed somehow. Shifted. The deep-set features were shadowed with depravity.

The earth dissolved as Christine realized what had happened.

"Oh God," she rasped. "Oh no. No . . ."

Jericho was possessed.

Desperately struggling to resist his savage strength, Christine felt herself being dragged to the altar, inch by terrifying inch. Past the statue of St. Michael, his Sword of Faith pointed at the ruined ceiling.

Jericho's sweating face steamed with unholy lust as he hauled her to the altar. Triumphantly, he forced her down in front of the crucifix.

"Jericho, no," Christine pleaded. "You've got to fight him. Please."

He ripped away her blouse, raw violence glazing his eyes as he pawed her pink-nippled breasts. "I know you," Christine pleaded. "You're stronger than him . . . That's why you came back for me. *Don't let him win!*"

Jericho's face came close to hers, careening between confusion and hate. Rage knotted his jaw and he squeezed Christine's soft neck. Muscles trembling, he battled the impulse to crush her throat. In stunned horror, Christine watched his face shift and ripple as if underwater. His features stretched into an obscene leer, then began to thicken into something loathsome . . . something unhuman. A sickening stench came from his clammy mouth as he tried to kiss her.

Her body shuddered with revulsion and she scratched and kicked wildly. *"Fight him Jericho!"* she screamed. *"Don't let him win!"*

For an instant the beast's hideous face melted back to human and Christine glimpsed Jericho's blurred features.

Abruptly Jericho wrenched back, eyes rolling madly toward the statue of St. Michael, then at Christine.

"Run!" Jericho groaned, mouth curling in an ugly grin.

Christine felt the ground drop away when Jericho's fingers released her.

Barely aware of what was happening, Christine saw Jericho turn, stagger, and jump. Her stunned brain was unable to process what happened.

Jericho took a stumbling leap and dove headlong onto St. Michael's marble sword—impaling himself. Oily with blood, the sword protruded obscenely from a gouging wound in his back.

Bellowing in demonic agony, he wriggled in midair like a huge insect.

Christine gaped uncomprehendingly, her emotions crashing like waves against rocks as she watched Jericho writhing in his death throes. Suddenly he went limp, arms flung back.

Sobbing, Christine staggered closer. Jericho's head sagged to one side, eyes closed, expression almost peaceful.

His eyes clicked open. With a bestial grin, he lunged free from the sword—and grabbed her arm. As he pulled her closer, the blood gushing from his wound become an oily black ooze. Whimpering with terror, Christine saw the ragged wound begin to heal.

And an unholy hunger pulsed through her belly.

A low rumbling bubbled up from beneath the church, swelling deeper and louder until it broke in a titanic wave, shaking the walls. As the rumbling flooded the church, a colossal thunderbolt cracked her consciousness— and Christine collapsed.

Dimly, from a great distance, chimes began to ring.

Then a faint chorus of human voices floated up in a familiar chant.

"NINE ... EIGHT ..."

Christine felt Jericho's weight pressing

down on her. Her eyes fluttered open and she saw his glazed, demonic features.

"... SEVEN ... SIX ..."

His ragged chest wound had nearly healed and Christine could feel his brutal strength pouring back as he pushed between her thighs.

"... FIVE ... FOUR ..."

Struggling, Christine heard his breath coming in quick, exhausted gasps and looked up. Jericho's face loomed over her, teeth clenched and eyes squeezed shut.

"... THREE.... TWO ...

Jericho opened his eyes and smiled.

"... ONE!"

"Arrrggghhhh," Jericho convulsed as the life force slid from his flesh like a hand being pulled from a glove.

A foul haze misted from beneath his skin, the fumes twisting into a grotesquely bestial form. It uttered an inhuman howl as the ground shattered open, erupting with flaming claws that tore the hideous presence to screeching shreds.

The pit opened wider as the fiery claws pulled their prey down into the great, sweltering maw. In that moment Christine glimpsed the yawning horror of lost souls. And knew the sorrow of God.

Suddenly a joyous noise broke through the discordant moans boiling through the chapel. Bells rang, whistles blew, and millions of voices came together in a single wish for humanity.

"Happy New Year!"

The next thousand years had begun. . . .

As if a dream, the swirling chaos evaporated into total silence. Except for the cheers drifting from Times Square and the wail of a distant siren, the chapel was quiet.

But for Christine, the lifeless body beside her was no dream. It was a living nightmare. "Jer! Jer!" she whimpered urgently, pawing at his bloody flesh. "Oh God, Jer . . . *Oh God, please, no!"*

Tears streamed down her face, falling on Jericho's cheek like salty rain.

A few glistening drops moistened his lips and his mouth moved.

Jericho's eyes opened, then closed again.

"Happy New Year . . . ," he murmured weakly.

Trembling, Chrstine ripped open his blood-soaked shirt. A jagged scar slashed his skin where St. Michael's sword had pierced his chest.

But the wound had healed.

Jericho lifted his head and looked at the scar creasing his chest. "The priest was right," he said quietly. "It was a test of faith."

"You would have given your life for me," Christine whispered.

Jericho grinned. "I thought I had."

She smiled, eyes smoldering with something deeply primal as she helped him stand. He put his arm around her and they began walking to the door.

It was then Christine saw the devastation around them: broken statues, shattered glass, splintered pews, and a thickening haze of smoke from a number of small fires. One confessional was blazing, igniting a large velvet wall hanging. And a cluster of hungry orange flames chewed at the altar.

By the time they pushed through the doors, the smoke had become a choking fog.

Outside it was New Year's Eve and beautifully snowing.

As Jericho and Christine staggered down the steps, fire sirens and revolving lights converged on the street below. Day-Glo-clad firemen rushed up the stairs past them and disappeared into the smoke billowing from the church.

"What happened?" one of the firemen asked.

Jericho cradled Christine in his arms and glanced down the street. A few blocks away in Times Square, the roaring crowds celebrated the turn of the century.

"There was a fire," he said tersely, walking past. "But I put it out," Jericho added, as he and Christine stumbled into the clear, snow-cooled night—and entered a new millennium.

Frank Lauria was born in Brooklyn, New York, and graduated from Manhattan College. He has traveled extensively and published fifteen novels, including five bestsellers and the novelizations of *Dark City*, *Mask of Zorro*, and *Alaska*. He has written articles and reviews for various magazines and is a published poet and songwriter. Mr. Lauria currently resides in San Francisco, where he teaches creative writing. A film project based on his Doctor Orient series is in development.

Read on for an excerpt from

AFTERBURN

A novel by Colin Harrison

Available from St. Martin's Press

CHINA CLUB, HONG KONG

He would survive. Yes, Charlie promised himself, he'd survive *this*, too—his ninth formal Chinese banquet in as many evenings, yet another bowl of shark-fin soup being passed to him by the endless waiters in red uniforms, who stood obsequiously against the silk wallpaper pretending not to hear the self-satisfied ravings of those they served. Except for his fellow *gweilos*—British Petroleum's Asia man, a mischievous German from Lufthansa, and two young American executives from Kodak and Citigroup—the other dozen men at the huge mahogany table were all Chinese. Mostly in their fifties, the men represented the big corporate players— Bank of Asia, Hong Kong Telecom, China Motors—and each, Charlie noted, had arrived at the age of cleverness. Of course, at fifty-eight he himself was old enough that no one should be able to guess what he was thinking unless he wanted them to, even Ellie. In his call to her that morning—it being evening in New York City—he'd tried not to sound too worried about their daughter Julia. "It's all going to be *fine*, sweetie," he'd promised, gazing out at the choppy haze of Hong Kong's harbor, where the heavy traffic of tankers and freighters pressed China's claim—everything from photocopiers to baseball caps flowing out into the world, everything from oil refineries to contact lenses flowing in. "She'll get pregnant, I'm sure," he'd told Ellie. But he wasn't sure. No, not at all. In fact, it looked as if it was going to be easier for him to build his electronics factory in Shanghai than for his daughter to hatch a baby.

"We gather in friendship," announced the Chinese host, Mr. Ming, the vice-chairman of the Bank of Asia. Having agreed to lend Charlie fifty-two million U.S. dollars to build his Shanghai factory, Mr. Ming in no way could be described as a friend; the relationship was one of overlord and indentured. But Charlie smiled along with the others as the banker stood and presented in high British English an analysis of southeastern China's economy that was so shallow, optimistic, and full of euphemism that no one, especially the central ministries in Beijing, might object. The Chinese executives nodded politely as Mr. Ming spoke, touching their napkins to their lips, smiling vaguely. Of course, they nursed secret worries—worries that corresponded to whether they were entrepreneurs (who had built shipping lines or real-estate empires or garment factories) or the managers of institutional power (who controlled billions of dollars not their own). And yet, Charlie decided, the men were finally more like one another than unlike; each long ago had learned to sell high (1997) and buy low (1998), and had passed the threshold of unspendable wealth, such riches conforming them in their behaviors; each owned more houses or paintings or Rolls-Royces than could be admired or used at once. Each played golf or tennis passably well; each possessed a forty-million-dollar yacht, or a forty-million-dollar home atop Victoria's Peak, or a forty-million-dollar wife. Each had a slender young Filipino or Russian or Czech mistress tucked away in one of Hong Kong's luxury apartment buildings—licking her lips if requested—or was betting against the Hong Kong dollar while insisting on its firmness—any of the costly mischief in which rich men indulge.

The men at the table, in fact, as much as any men, sat as money incarnate, particularly the American dollar, the euro, and the

Japanese yen—all simultaneously, and all hedged against fluctuations of the others. But although the men were money, money was not them; money assumed any shape or color or politics, it could be fire or stone or dream, it could summon armies or bind atoms, and, indifferent to the sufferings of the mortal soul, it could leave or arrive at any time. And on this exact night, Charlie thought, setting his ivory chopsticks neatly upon the lacquered plate, he could see that although money had assumed the shapes of the men in the room, it existed in differing densities and volumes and brightnesses. Whereas Charlie was a man of perhaps thirty or thirty-three million dollars of wealth, that sum amounted to shoe-shine change in the present company. No, sir, money, in *that* room, in *that* moment, was understood as inconsequential in sums less than one hundred million dollars, and of political importance only when five times more. Money, in fact, found its greatest compression and gravity in the form of the tiny man sitting silently across from Charlie—Sir Henry Lai, the Oxford-educated Chinese gambling mogul, owner of a fleet of jet-foil ferries, a dozen hotels, and most of the casinos of Macao and Vietnam. Worth billions—and billions more.

But, Charlie wondered, perhaps he was wrong. He could think of one shape that money had not *yet* assumed, although quite a bit of it had been spent, perhaps a hundred thousand dollars in all. Money animated the dapper Chinese businessman across from him, but could it arrive in the world as Charlie's own grandchild? This was the question he feared most, this was the question that had eaten at him and at Ellie for years now, and which would soon be answered: In a few hours, Julia would tell them once and forever if she was capable of having a baby.

She had suffered through cycle upon cycle of disappointment—hundreds of shots of fertility drugs followed by the needle-recovery of the eggs, the inspection of the eggs, the selection of the eggs, the insemination of the eggs, the implantation of the eggs, the anticipation of the eggs. She'd been trying for seven years. Now Julia, a woman of only thirty-five, a little gray already salting her hair, was due to get the final word. At 11:00 a.m. Manhattan time, she'd sit in her law office and be told the results of this, the last in-vitro attempt. Her *ninth.* Three more than the doctor preferred to do. Seven more than the insurance company would pay for. Good news would be that one of the reinserted fertilized eggs had decided to cling to the wall of Julia's uterus. Bad news: There was no chance of conception; egg donorship or adoption must now be considered. And if *that* was the news, well then, that was really goddamn something. It would mean not just that his only daughter was heartbroken, but that, genetically speaking, he, Charlie Ravich, was finished, that his own fishy little spermatozoa—one of which, wiggling into Ellie's egg a generation prior, had become his daughter—had run aground, that he'd come to the end of the line; that, in a sense, he was already dead.

And now, as if mocking his very thoughts, came the fish, twenty pounds of it, head still on, its eyes cooked out and replaced with flowered radishes, its mouth agape in macabre broiled amusement. Charlie looked at his plate. He always lost weight in China, undone by the soy and oils and crusted skin of birds, the rich liverish stink of turtle meat. All that duck tongue and pig ear and fish lip. Expensive as hell, every meal. And carrying with it the odor of doom.

Then the conversation turned, as it also did so often in Shanghai and Beijing, to the question of America's mistreatment of the Chinese. "What I do not understand are the American senators," Sir Henry Lai was saying in his softly refined voice. "They say they *understand* that we only want for China to be China." Every syllable was flawless English, but of course Lai also spoke Mandarin and Cantonese. Sir Henry Lai was reported to be in serious talks with Gaming Technologies, the huge American gambling and hotel conglomerate that clutched big pieces of Las Vegas, the Mississippi casino towns, and Atlantic City. Did Sir Henry know when China would allow Western-style casinos to be built within its borders? Certainly he knew the right officials in Beijing, and perhaps this was reason enough that GT's stock price had ballooned up seventy percent in the last three months as Sir Henry's interest in the company had become known. Lai smiled benignly. Then frowned. "These senators say that all they want is for international trade to progress without interruption, and then they go back to Congress and raise their fists and call China all kinds of names. Is this not true?"

The others nodded sagely, apparently giving consideration, but not ignoring whatever delicacy remained pinched in their chopsticks.

"Wait, I have an answer to that," announced the young fellow from Citigroup. "Mr. Lai, I trust we may speak frankly here. You need to remember that the American senators are full of—excuse my language— full of shit. When they're standing up on the Senate floor saying all of this stuff, this means nothing, *absolutely* nothing!"

"Ah, this is very difficult for the Chinese

people to understand." Sir Henry scowled.
"In China we believe our leaders. So we become scared when we see American senators complaining about China."

"You're being coy with us, Mr. Lai," interrupted Charlie, looking up with a smile, "for we—or some of us—know that you have visited the United States dozens of times and have met many U.S. senators personally." Not to mention a few Third World dictators. He paused, while amusement passed into Lai's dark eyes. "Nonetheless," Charlie continued, looking about the table, "for the others who have not enjoyed Mr. Lai's deep friendships with American politicians, I would have to say my colleague here is right. The speeches in the American Senate are pure grandstanding. They're made for the American public—"

"The *bloodthirsty* American public, you mean!" interrupted the Citigroup man, who, Charlie suddenly understood, had drunk too much. "Those old guys up there know most voters can't find China on a globe. That's no joke. It's shocking, the American ignorance of China."

"We shall have to educate your people," Sir Henry Lai offered diplomatically, apparently not wishing the stridency of the conversation to continue. He gave a polite, cold-blooded laugh.

"But it is, yes, my understanding that the Americans could sink the Chinese Navy in several days?" barked the German from Lufthansa.

"That may be true," answered Charlie, "but sooner or later the American people are going to recognize the hemispheric primacy of China, that—"

"Wait, wait!" Lai interrupted good-naturedly. "You agree with our German friend about the Chinese Navy?"

The question was a direct appeal to the nationalism of the other Chinese around the table.

"Can the U.S. Air Force destroy the Chinese Navy in a matter of days?" repeated Charlie. "Yes. Absolutely yes."

Sir Henry Lai smiled. "You are knowledgeable about these topics, Mr."—he glanced down at the business cards arrayed in front of his plate—"Mr. Ravich. Of the Teknetrix Corporation, I see. What do you know about war, Mr. Ravich?" he asked. "Please, tell me. I am curious."

The Chinese billionaire stared at him with eyebrows lifted, face a smug, florid mask, and if Charlie had been younger or genuinely insulted, he might have recalled aloud his war years before becoming a businessman, but he understood that generally it was to one's advantage not to appear to have an advantage. And anyway, the conversation was merely a form of sport: Lai didn't give a good goddamn about the Chinese Navy, which he probably despised; what he cared about was whether or not he should soon spend eight hundred million dollars on GT stock—play the corporation that played the players.

But Lai pressed. "What do you know about this?"

"Just what I read in the papers," Charlie replied with humility.

"See? There! I tell you!" Lai eased back in his silk suit, running a fat little palm over his thinning hair. "This is a very dangerous problem, my friends. People say many things about China and America, but they have no direct knowledge, no real—"

Mercifully, the boys in red uniforms and brass buttons began setting down spoons and bringing around coffee. Charlie excused himself and headed for the gentlemen's restroom. Please, God, he thought, it's a small favor, really. One egg clinging to a warm pink wall. He and Ellie should have had another child, should have at least tried, after Ben. Ellie had been forty-two. Too much grief at the time, too late now.

In the men's room, a sarcophagus of black and silver marble, he nodded at the wizened Chinese attendant, who stood up with alert servility. Charlie chose the second stall and locked the heavy marble door behind him. The door and walls extended in smooth veined slabs from the floor to within a foot of the ceiling. The photo-electric eye over the toilet sensed his movement and the bowl flushed prematurely. He was developing an old man's interest in his bowels. He shat then, with the private pleasure of it. He was starting to smell Chinese to himself. Happened on every trip to the East.

And then, as he finished, he heard the old attendant greeting another man in Cantonese.

"Evening, sir."

"Yes."

The stall door next to Charlie's opened, shut, was locked. The man was breathing as if he had hurried. Then came some loud coughing, an oddly tiny splash, and the muffled silky sound of the man slumping heavily against the wall he shared with Charlie.

"Sir?" The attendant knocked on Charlie's door. "You open door?"

Charlie buckled his pants and slid the lock free. The old man's face loomed close, eyes large, breath stinking.

"Not me!" Charlie said. "The next one!"

"No have key! Climb!" The old attendant pushed past Charlie, stepped up on the toilet seat, and stretched high against the glassy marble. His bony hands pawed the stone uselessly. Now the man in the adjacent stall was moaning in Chinese, begging for help. Charlie pulled the attendant down and stood on the toilet seat himself. With his arms outstretched he could reach the top of the wall, and he sucked in a breath and hoisted himself. Grimacing, he pulled himself up high enough so that his nose touched the top edge of the wall. But before being able to look over, he fell back.

"Go!" he ordered the attendant. "Get help, get a key!"

The man in the stall groaned, his respiration a song of pain. Charlie stepped up on the seat again, this time jumping exactly at the moment he pulled with his arms, and then *yes*, he was up, right up there, hooking one leg over the wall, his head just high enough to peer down and see Sir Henry Lai slumped on the floor, his face a rictus of purpled flesh, his pants around his ankles, a piss stain spreading across his silk boxers. His hands clutched weakly at his tie, the veins of his neck swollen like blue pencils. His eyes, not squeezed shut but open, stared up at the underside of the spotless toilet bowl, into which, Charlie could see from above, a small silver pillbox had fallen, top open, the white pills inside of it scattered and sunk and melting away.

"Hang on," breathed Charlie. "They're coming. Hang on." He tried to pull himself through the opening between the wall and ceiling, but it was no good; he could get his head through but not his shoulders or torso. Now Sir Henry Lai coughed rhythmically, as if uttering some last strange code—"Haa-cah . . . Haaa! Haaa!"—and convulsed, his eyes peering in pained wonderment straight into Charlie's, then widening as his mouth filled with a reddish soup of undigested shrimp and pigeon and turtle that surged up over his lips and ran down both of his cheeks before draining back into his windpipe. He was too far gone to cough the vomit out of his lungs, and the tension in his hands eased— he was dying of a heart attack and asphyxiation at the same moment.

The attendant hurried back in with Sir Henry's bodyguard. They pounded on the stall door with something, cracking the marble. The beautiful veined stone broke away in pieces, some falling on Sir Henry Lai's shoes. Charlie looked back at his face. Henry Lai was dead.

The men stepped into the stall and Charlie knew he was of no further use. He dropped back to the floor, picked up his jacket, and walked out of the men's restroom, expecting a commotion outside. A waiter sailed past;

the assembled businessmen didn't know what had happened.

Mr. Ming watched him enter.

"I must leave you," Charlie said graciously. "I'm very sorry. My daughter is due to call me tonight with important news."

"Good news, I trust."

The only news bankers liked. "Perhaps. She's going to tell me if she is pregnant."

"I hope you are blessed." Mr. Ming smiled, teeth white as Ellie's estrogen pills.

Charlie nodded warmly. "We're going to build a terrific factory, too. Should be on-line by the end of the year."

"We are scheduled for lunch in about two weeks in New York?"

"Absolutely," said Charlie. Every minute now was important.

Mr. Ming bent closer, his voice softening. "And you will tell me then about the quadport transformer you are developing?"

His secret new datacom switch, which would smoke the competition? No. "Yes." Charlie smiled. "Sure deal."

"Excellent," pronounced Mr. Ming. "Have a good flight."

The stairs to the lobby spiraled along backlit cabinets of jade dragons and coral boats and who cared what else. Don't run, Charlie told himself, don't appear to be in a hurry. In London, seven hours behind Hong Kong,

the stock market was still open. He pointed
to his coat for the attendant then nodded at
the first taxi waiting outside.

"FCC," he told the driver.

"Foreign Correspondents' Club?"

"Right away."

It was the only place open at night in
Hong Kong where he knew he could get access to a Bloomberg box—that magical electronic screen that displayed every stock and
bond price in every market around the globe.
He pulled out his cell phone and called his
broker in London.

"Jane, this is Charlie Ravich," he said
when she answered. "I want to set up a huge
put play. Drop everything."

"This is not like you."

"This is not like anything. Sell all my Mi-
crosoft now at the market price, sell all the
Ford, the Merck, all the Lucent. Market orders all of them. Please, right now, before
London closes."

"All right now, for the tape, you are request-
ing we sell eight thousand shares of—"

"Yes, yes, I agree," he blurted.

Jane was off the line, getting another broker to carry out the orders. "Zoom-de-
doom," she said when she returned. "Let it
rip."

"This is going to add up to about one-point-oh-seven million," he said. "I'm buying puts on Gaming Technologies, the gambling company. It's American but trades in London."

"Yes." Now her voice held interest. "*Yes*."

"How many puts of GT can I buy with that?"

She was shouting orders to her clerks. "Wait . . ." she said. "Yes? Very good. I have your account on my screen . . ." He heard keys clicking. "We have . . . one million seventy thousand, U.S., plus change. Now then, Gaming Technologies is selling at sixty-six even a share—"

"How many puts can I buy with one-point-oh-seven?"

"Oh, I would say a huge number, Charlie."

"How many?"

"About . . . one-point-six million shares."

"That's huge."

"You want to protect that bet?" she asked.

"No."

"If you say so."

"Buy the puts, Jane."

"I am, Charlie, *please*. The price is stable. Yes, take this one . . ." she was saying to a clerk. "Give me puts on GT at market, immediately. Yes. One-point-six million at the money. *Yes*. At the money." The line was silent a moment. "You sure, Charlie?"

"This is a bullet to the moon, Jane."

"Biggest bet of your life, Charlie?"

"Oh, Jane, not even close."

Outside his cab a silky red Rolls glided past. "Got it?" he asked.

"Not quite. You going to tell me the play, Charlie?"

"When it goes through, Jane."

"We'll get the order back in a minute or two."

Die on the shitter, Charlie thought. Could happen to anyone. Happened to Elvis Presley, matter of fact.

"Charlie?"

"Yes."

"We have your puts. One-point-six million, GT, at the price of sixty-six." He heard the keys clicking.

"*Now* tell me?" Jane pleaded.

"I will," Charlie said. "Just give me the confirmation for the tape."

While she repeated the price and the volume of the order, he looked out the window to see how close the taxi was to the FCC. He'd first visited the club in 1970, when it was full of drunken television and newspaper journalists, CIA people, Army intelligence, retired British admirals who had gone native, and crazy Texans provisioning the war; since then, the rest of Hong Kong had been built up and torn down and built up all over again, but the FCC still stood, tucked away on a side street.

"I just want to get my times right," Charlie told Jane when she was done. "It's now a few minutes after 9:00 p.m. on Tuesday in Hong Kong. What time are you in London?"

"Just after 2:00 p.m."

"London markets are open about an hour more?"

"Yes," Jane said.

"New York starts trading in half an hour."

"Yes."

"I need you to stay in your office and handle New York for me."

She sighed. "I'm due to pick up my son from school."

"Need a car, a new car?"

"Everybody needs a new car."

"Just stay there a few more hours, Jane. You can pick out a Mercedes tomorrow morning and charge it to my account."

"You're a charmer, Charlie."

"I'm serious. Charge my account."

"Okay, will you *please* tell me?"

Of course he would, but because he needed to get the news moving. "Sir Henry Lai just died. Maybe fifteen minutes ago."

"Sir Henry Lai . . ."

"The Macao gambling billionaire who was in deep talks with GT—"

"Yes! Yes!" Jane cried. "Are you sure?"

"Yes."

"It's not just a rumor?"

"Jane, you don't trust old Charlie Ravich?"

"It's dropping! Oh! Down to sixty-four," she cried. "There it goes! There go ninety thousand shares! Somebody else got the word out! Sixty-three and a—Charlie, oh Jesus, you beat it by maybe a minute."

He told her he'd call again shortly and stepped out of the cab into the club, a place so informal that the clerk just gave him a nod; people strode in all day long to have drinks in the main bar. Inside sat several dozen men and women drinking and smoking, many of them American and British journalists, others small-time local businessmen who long ago had slid into alcoholism, burned out, boiled over, or given up.

He ordered a whiskey and sat down in front of the Bloomberg box, fiddling with it until he found the correct menu for real-time London equities. He was up millions and the New York Stock Exchange had not even opened yet. Ha! The big American shareholders of GT, or, more particularly, their analysts and advisers and market watchers, most of them punks in their thirties, were still tying their shoes and kissing the mirror and soon—very soon!—they'd be saying hello to the receptionist sitting down at their screens. Minutes away! When they found out

that Sir Henry Lai had died in the China
Club in Hong Kong at 8:45 p.m. Hong Kong
time, they would assume, Charlie hoped,
that because Lai ran an Asian-style, family-
owned corporation, and because as its patri-
arch he dominated its governance, any
possible deal with GT was off, indefinitely.
They would then reconsider the price of GT,
still absurdly stratospheric, and dump it fast.
Maybe. He ordered another drink, then
called Jane.

"GT is down five points," she told him.
"New York is about to open."

"But I don't see *panic* yet. Where's the volume selling?"

"You're not going to see it here, not with
New York opening. I'll be sitting right here."

"Excellent, Jane. Thank you."

"Not at all. Call me when you're ready to
close it out."

He hung up, looked into the screen. The
real-time price of GT was hovering at fifty-
nine dollars a share. No notice had moved
over the information services yet. Not
Bloomberg, not Reuters.

He went back to the bar, pushed his way
past a couple of journalists.

"Another?" the bartender asked.

"Yes, sir. A double," he answered loudly.
"I just got very bad news."

"Sorry to hear that." The bartender did not look up.

"Yes." Charlie nodded solemnly. "Sir Henry Lai died tonight, heart attack at the China Club. A terrible thing." He slid one hundred Hong Kong dollars across the bar. Several of the journalists peered at him.

"Pardon me," asked one, a tall Englishman with a riot of red hair. "Did I hear you say Sir Henry Lai has *died*?"

Charlie nodded. "Not an hour ago. I just happened to be standing there, at the China Club." He tasted his drink. "Please excuse me."

He returned to the Bloomberg screen. The Englishman, he noticed, had slipped away to a pay phone in the corner. The New York Stock Exchange, casino to the world, had been open a minute. He waited. Three, four, five minutes. And then, finally, came what he'd been waiting for, Sir Henry Lai's epitaph: GT's price began shrinking as its volume exploded—half a million shares, price fifty-eight, fifty-six, two million shares, fifty-five and a half. He watched. Four million shares now. The stock would bottom and bounce. He'd wait until the volume slowed. At fifty-five and a quarter he pulled his phone out of his pocket and called Jane. At fifty-five and seven-eighths he bought back the shares he'd sold at sixty-six, for a profit of a bit more than ten dollars a share. Major money. Sixteen million before taxes. Big money. Real money. Elvis money.

It was almost eleven when he arrived back at his hotel. The Sikh doorman, a vestige from the days of the British Empire, nodded a greeting. Inside the immense lobby a piano player pushed along a little tune that made Charlie feel mournful, and he sat down in one of the deep chairs that faced the harbor. So much ship traffic, hundreds of barges and freighters and, farther out, the supertankers. To the east sprawled the new airport—they had filled in the ocean there, hiring half of all the world's deep-water dredging equipment to do it. History in all this. He was looking at ships moving across the dark waters, but he might as well be looking at the twenty-first century itself, looking at his own countrymen who could not find factory jobs. The poor fucks had no idea what was coming at them, not a clue. China was a juggernaut, an immense, seething mass. It was building aircraft carriers, it was buying Taiwan. It shrugged off turmoil in Western stock markets. Currency fluctuations, inflation, deflation, volatility—none of these things compared to the fact that China had eight hundred and fifty million people under the age of thirty-five. They wanted everything Americans now took for granted, including the right to piss on the shoes of any other country in the world.

But ha! There might be some consolation! He pushed back in the seat, slipped on his half-frame glasses, and did the math on a hotel napkin. After commissions and taxes, his evening's activities had netted him close to eight million dollars—a sum grotesque not so much for its size but for the speed and ease with which he had seized it—two phone calls!—and, most of all, for its mockery of human toil. Well, it was a grotesque world now. He'd done nothing but understand what the theorists called a market inefficiency and what everyone else knew as inside information. If he was a ghoul, wrenching dollars from Sir Henry Lai's vomit-filled mouth, then at least the money would go to good use. He'd put all of it in a bypass trust for Julia's child. The funds could pay for clothes and school and pediatrician's bills and whatever else. It could pay for a *life*. He remembered his father buying used car tires from the garage of the Minnesota Highway Patrol for a dollar-fifty. No such thing as steel-belted radials in 1956. You cross borders of time, and if people don't come with you, you lose them and they you. Now it was an age when a fifty-eight-year-old American executive could net eight million bucks by watching a man choke to death. His father would never have understood it, and he suspected that Ellie couldn't, either. Not really. There was something in her head lately. Maybe it was because of Julia, but maybe not. She bought expensive vegetables she let rot in the refrigerator, she took Charlie's blood-pressure pills by mistake, she left the phone off the hook. He wanted to be patient with her but could not. She drove him nuts.

He sat in the hotel lobby for an hour more, reading every article in the *International Herald Tribune*. Finally, at midnight, he decided not to wait for Julia's call and pulled his phone from his pocket and dialed her Manhattan office.

"Tell me, sweetie," he said once he got past the secretary.

"Oh, Daddy . . ."

"Yes?"

A pause. And then she cried.

"Okay, now," he breathed, closing his eyes. "Okay."

She gathered herself. "All right. I'm fine. It's okay. You don't have to have children to have a fulfilling life. I can handle this."

"Tell me what they said."

"They said I'll probably never have my own children, they think the odds are—all I know is that I'll never hold my *own* baby, never, just something I'll never, ever do."

"Oh, sweetie."

"We really thought it was going to work. You know? I've had a lot of faith with this thing. They have these new egg-handling techniques, makes them glue to the walls of the uterus."

They were both silent a moment.

"I mean, you kind of expect that *technology* will work," Julia went on, her voice thoughtful. "They can clone human beings—they can do all of these things and they can't—" She stopped.

The day had piled up on him, and he was trying to remember all that Julia had explained to him about eggs and tubes and hormone levels. "Sweetie," he tried, "the problem is not exactly the eggs?"

"My eggs are pretty lousy, *also*. You're wondering if we could put *my* egg in another woman, right?"

"No, not—well, maybe yes," he sighed.

"They don't think it would work. The eggs aren't that viable."

"And your tubes—"

She gave a bitter laugh. "I'm *barren*, Daddy. I can't make good eggs, and I can't hatch eggs, mine or anyone else's."

He watched the lights of a tanker slide along the oily water outside. "I know it's too early to start discussing adoption, but—"

"He doesn't want to do it. At least he says he won't," she sobbed.

"Wait, sweetie," Charlie responded, hearing her despair, "Brian is just— Adopting a child is—"

"No, no, *no*, Daddy, Brian doesn't *want* a little Guatemalan baby or a Lithuanian baby or anybody else's baby but his own. It's about his own goddamn *penis*. If it doesn't come out of *his* penis, then it's no good."

Her husband's view made sense to him, but he couldn't say that now. "Julia, I'm sure Brian—"

"I *would* have adopted a little baby a year ago, two years ago! But I put up with all this shit, all these hormones and needles in my butt and doctors pushing things up me, *for him*. And now those *years* are— Oh, I'm sorry, Daddy, I have a client. I'll talk to you when you come back. I'm very— I have a lot of calls here. Bye."

He listened to the satellite crackle in the phone, then the announcement in Chinese to hang up. His flight was at eight the next morning, New York seventeen hours away, and as always, he wanted to get home, and yet didn't, for as soon as he arrived, he would miss China. The place got to him, like a recurrent dream, or a fever—forced possibilities into his mind, whispered ideas he didn't want to hear. Like the eight million. It was perfectly legal yet also a kind of contraband. If he wanted, Ellie would never see the money; she had long since ceased to be interested in his financial gamesmanship, so long as there was enough money for Belgian chocolates for the elevator man at Christmas, fresh flowers twice a week, and the farmhouse in Tuscany. But like a flash of unexpected lightning, the new money illuminated certain questions begging for years at the edge of his consciousness. He had been rich for a long time, but now he was rich enough to fuck with fate. Had he been waiting for this moment? Yes, waiting until he knew about Julia, waiting until he was certain.

He called Martha Wainwright, his personal lawyer. "Martha, I've finally decided to do it," he said when she answered.

"Oh, Christ, Charlie, don't tell me that."

"Yes. Fact, I just made a little extra money in a stock deal. Makes the whole thing that much easier."

"Don't do it, Charlie."

"I just got the word from my daughter, Martha. If she could have children, it would be a different story."

"This is bullshit, Charlie. Male bullshit."

"Is that your legal opinion or your political one?"

"I'm going to argue with you when you get back," she warned.

"Fine—I expect that. For now, please just put the ad in the magazines and get all the documents ready."

"I think you are a complete jerk for doing this."

"We understand things differently, Martha."

"Yes, because *you* are addicted to testosterone."

"Most men are, Martha. That's what makes us such assholes."

"You having erection problems, Charlie? Is *that* what this is about?"

"You got the wrong guy, Martha. My dick is like an old dog."

"How's that? Sleeps all the time?"

"Slow but dependable," he lied. "Comes when you call it."

She sighed. "Why don't you just let me hire a couple of strippers to sit on your face? That'd be *infinitely* cheaper."

"That's not what this is about, Martha."

"Oh, Charlie."

"I'm serious, I really am."

"Ellie will be terribly hurt."

"She doesn't need to know."

"She'll find out, believe me. They always do." Martha's voice was distraught. "She'll find out you're advertising for a woman to have your baby, and then she'll just flip out, Charlie."

"Not if you do your job well."

"You really this afraid of death?"

"Not death, Martha, oblivion. Oblivion is the thing that really kills me."

"You're better than this, Charlie."

"The ad, just put in the ad."

He hung up. In a few days the notice would sneak into the back pages of New York's weeklies, a discreet little box in the personals, specifying the arrangement he sought and the benefits he offered. Martha would begin screening the applications. He'd see who responded. You never knew who was out there.

He sat quietly then, a saddened but prosperous American exccutive in a good suit, his gray hair neatly barbered, and followed the ships out on the water. One of the hotel's Eurasian prostitutes watched him from across the lobby as she sipped a watered-down drink. Perhaps sensing a certain opportune grief in the stillness of his posture, she slipped over the marble floor and bent close to ask softly if he would like some company, but he shook his head no—although not, she would see, without a bit of lonely gratitude, not without a quick hungered glance of his eyes into hers—and he continued to sit calmly, with that stillness to him. Noticing this, one would have thought not that in one evening he had watched a man die, or made millions, or lied to his banker, or worried that his flesh might never go forward, but that he was privately toasting what was left of the century, wondering what revelation it might yet bring.

Six-year-old Paul Haines watches as two older boys dive into a coastal river...and don't come up. His mother, Carolyn, a charter boat captain on the Mississippi Gulf Coast, finds herself embroiled in the tragedy to an extent she could never have imagined.

Carolyn joins with marine biologist Alan Freeman in the hunt for a creature that is terrorizing the waters along the Gulf Coast. But neither of them could have envisioned exactly what kind of danger they are facing.

Only one man knows what this creature is, and how it has come into the shallows. And his secret obsession with it will force him, as well as Paul, Carolyn and Alan, into a race against time...and a race toward death.

EXTINCT

by Charles Wilson

"Eminently plausible, chilling in its detail, and highly entertaining straight through to its finale."
—DR. DEAN A. DUNN, Professor of Oceanography and Paleontology, University of Southern Mississippi

"With his taut tales and fast words, Charles Wilson will be around for a long time. I hope so."
—JOHN GRISHAM

THE SILENCE OF THE LAMBS

THE ELECTRIFYING BESTSELLER BY
THOMAS HARRIS
AUTHOR OF *RED DRAGON* AND *HANNIBAL*

"THRILLERS DON'T COME
ANY BETTER THAN THIS."
—CLIVE BARKER

"HARRIS IS QUITE SIMPLY THE BEST
SUSPENSE NOVELIST WORKING TODAY."
—THE WASHINGTON POST

THE SILENCE OF THE LAMBS
Thomas Harris
0-312-92458-5___ $7.99 U.S.___ $9.99 Can.